The Remarkable Story of
Paul the Apostle

The Remarkable Story of
Paul the Apostle

Siegwart Knijpenga

Floris
Books

Translated by Philip Mees
Illustrations by Ardan Heerkens

Cover illustration: *Saint Paul* by Bartolomeo Montagna

First published in Dutch as *Paulus von Tarsus*
by De Christengemeenschap, Netherlands in 2018
First published in English by Floris Books, Edinburgh in 2021
© 2018 Siegwart Knijpenga
English version © 2021 Floris Books

 Also available as an eBook

British Library CIP data available
ISBN 978-178250-736-9
Printed in Great Britain by Bell & Bain, Ltd

 Floris Books supports sustainable forest management by
printing this book on materials made from wood that
comes from responsible sources and reclaimed material

Contents

1: Growing Up in Tarsus   7

2: A Light in the East   15

3: Arriving in Jerusalem   22

4: Saul's Long Search for the Messiah   28

5: Damascus   36

6: Saul Returns to Jerusalem   49

7: Saul Becomes Paul   53

8: The First Christians   63

9: Paul's First Great Journey   70

10: Everything is Made New   86

11: Paul's Second Great Journey   90

12: The Unknown God   103

13: Paul's Third Great Journey   114

14: Paul is Arrested   122

15: Paul on Trial   129

16: Voyage to Rome   139

17: The Eternal City   146

Maps   152

Glossary   156

1: Growing Up in Tarsus

I

In his workshop, Saul's father, Joachim, was making a large tent. He had bought goat skins from the tanner and washed them in a big tub. When they were dry he had measured the pieces he needed. He marked them with chalk and called over his ten-year-old son, Saul. Later in life, Saul would choose to be called Paul, but when he was young he was known as Saul.

Joachim gave his son the knife and placed the first skin flat on the big cutting table. While he stretched the leather with both hands, Saul, holding his breath and pressing his lips together, pulled the blade slowly and carefully through the leather along the chalk line. Then Joachim turned the skin and Saul, already feeling a little less tense, cut the next line.

"You're doing well, you could even press a little less, but keep the blade on the line. Right, now the third cut. Keep the leather stretched with your left hand and cut only with the right hand. Yes, excellent! Be careful with the last piece – I can't get a good grip on the last edge."

With a sigh of relief, Saul put the knife down. He watched as his father flattened the leather on the table and checked it with his measuring stick. "Look," said Joachim, "exactly right. And now the next one."

Saul drew a deep breath and wiped the sweat from his forehead. His father marked up another skin and Saul set to work with the knife. Already it felt easier. In this way, piece after piece was cut to size that morning until Joachim said, "We have enough."

"What comes next?" Saul wanted to know.

"From these pieces I will make the roof. I have to sew them together. Then come the sides. I need to attach thick pieces of cowhide where the poles and lines go through, otherwise the tent will leak. Then we will make the poles, the lines and the pegs. It will take me another week."

"I want to help you," said Saul.

Joachim laughed and said, "You are already becoming a tentmaker and that's a good thing. But do you know your teacher has very different plans for you? He says that you're a quick learner and that one day, when you are finished with school, you might even become a rabbi or a scholar of the Law, just like him. What do you think of that?"

Saul fell silent, daunted by the thought. But his teacher, Athenodorus, was wise and Saul trusted him.

"But how would I do that?" he asked. "Would I go to the Rabbinical school here in Tarsus?"

Before his father could answer, Saul's mother, Dina, appeared in the doorway of the workshop. A rounded bump was beginning to show beneath her tunic. Soon, Saul would have a younger brother or sister. He hadn't decided yet which he would prefer, but he was excited.

"Saul, dinner is almost ready, but I need to cure some more olives," she said. "Could you go and pick them for me?" Dina passed her son a basket.

Saul liked the orchard in the garden behind their house. He knew that the old tree against the rear fence had ripe fruit, and he searched among the tangle of low-hanging branches for the best olives.

While he searched, Saul considered the tree. It was odd: the trunk was very old and had decayed in the middle; only the gnarled and twisted outer layer was still standing. But his father had grafted at least ten other branches onto it and they were continuing to grow. His father was clever choosing the side that caught the most sun – the fruit on that branch was getting better every year.

"Saul!" his mother called.

Saul quickly filled his basket with the firm, green olives and took them to the kitchen.

"Were you dreaming again?" his mother asked. "We're hungry. But the basket is nice and full."

After the meal, Saul stayed in his seat, gazing out of the window.

"That olive tree of ours is old and young at the same time," he said. "Inside it is dying but on the outside it becomes new again. How long can that go on for? And how long ago was the tree completely new?"

"It was already old when I came here," Dina said.

Joachim agreed. "I was born here, and I have always seen it as it is now."

"Well, the olives are delicious," Saul laughed as he popped the last one into his mouth. "Anyway, I'm off to the waterfront to meet Kyrill."

But Joachim said, "Go first to the harbour, and ask the captain if he intends to stop at Seleucia when he sails. If so, ask him if he can take a tent for us."

"Yes, Father."

Saul ran off. His mother watched him disappear as she washed the dishes. "The things that boy comes out with. His teacher is right about seeing a rabbi in him," she said to herself.

Saul ran to the port where the captain was standing by the gang plank that led onto his ship, waving a welcome with his cap. A little out of breath, Saul asked if the captain was stopping at Seleucia. The captain nodded.

"We have another tent for you to take, a big one, and I helped with it." Saul said. "It's beautiful."

"I'm sure it is," the captain said. "Bring it tomorrow, late in the afternoon."

"Yes, Captain. And if you need someone to help you on your journey, I'd be happy to come along."

The captain laughed. "Why are you so eager to get away from here? Don't you realise what a wonderful place this is? People come from all over the world to trade here. No other country has farmland that produces so much fruit, and let's not forget the cedar and olive trees growing on the Taurus Mountains. The wood from those trees is used in other countries to build not only houses, but also castles and temples. And there is so much history here too. Not far from here is where Alexander the Great defeated the Persians. After that, people from Macedonia and Greece came here bringing their language and their culture. But just as important was the arrival of the Romans. The emperor Pompey made Tarsus the capital of this part of his empire, and he gave Roman citizenship to every inhabitant. It was here that Princess Cleopatra arrived from Egypt in her magnificent boat, and so bewitched the great Antony with her beauty that he made her his wife. Just

imagine, all of that, happening right here on your door-step. Why would you want to leave?"

"Because I want to travel the world like you do and have adventures."

The captain laughed again. "I see. It's adventure you want is it? In that case it's lucky you're a Roman citizen. You can go anywhere in the empire you like. You need only say you're a Roman citizen and people will look up to you. You speak Latin, Greek and Hebrew, so you'll have no difficulty talking to people and getting into adventures. And Tarsus is a good place to find a boat, they go in all directions from here. But first you must finish school."

"I suppose you're right," Saul said.

"There's no 'suppose' about it," the captain replied. "Be patient, lad. Your time will come."

Saul thanked the captain and said he would see him tomorrow afternoon when he came with his father to load the tent. Then, his head still spinning with all the glorious things the captain had said, Saul wandered off along the waterfront in search of his friend Kyrill.

II

A few months later, Saul was woken early one morning by his father. Joachim sat on the edge of Saul's bed, looking down at him with a broad smile, his eyes shining with excitement.

"My boy, the baby was born last night."

Saul sat up, rubbing his eyes. "And?"

"It's a girl. A sweet, beautiful little girl."

"Oh."

"She will be fun to play with later on," said Joachim. "She will have to learn a lot first, of course. You could help her with that."

"Can I see her?" Saul asked.

Joachim took him by the hand and led him through into his parents' bedroom. Saul was pleased to see his mother awake and sitting up in bed. She smiled when she saw him and waved him over, placing a finger against her lips for him to be quiet. Next to the bed was a small cot. Saul peered over the edge. Lying in the bottom, wrapped in a blanket, was his little sister, fast asleep. She was so small and beautiful and Saul felt a huge surge of love for her, like the sea rushing up the shore. He stared at her, amazed and utterly speechless.

"Was I also like that?" he asked in a soft voice.

"You were just a little bigger," his mother replied in a whisper, "but not much, for you were born earlier than we expected. I guess you were in a hurry."

"And did I also sleep a lot?"

"Yes, even longer than children who are born on time. That is usually the case."

Saul gazed at his sister for a while in silence.

"But she can't play with me yet?"

"Not yet," his father said. "But there's lots you can do to help her. She will have to learn how to wash and get dressed, how to eat and even how to talk. You can help her with that. Your mother and I will need you, because we will have a lot of other things to do."

"What's her name?" Saul asked.

"Esther," his mother said. "After the brave woman who saved our people from the Persian king."

Saul turned back to his sister.

"Esther," he said, softly, trying out the name. He smiled and made a small sound of satisfaction. It was perfect.

In the time that followed, Saul would be busy with all the many things that he wanted to learn and do, but he would always help his sister if she needed something. If anyone was unkind to her they would have him to deal with, for although Saul was small in stature, he was fearless. He would do anything for his sister. And many years later, Esther would repay his kindness, when, like her namesake, she helped her brother escape danger.

But all of that was still a long way off. For now, the young Saul was happy just to stand by the cot, gazing in fascination at his little sister as she slept.

2: A Light in the East

I

A week before he turned twelve, Saul's father came to him and said, "It's time you learnt how to weave."

They went to the workshop where Joachim kept the large loom.

"This bench loom is too big for you at the moment," he said. "We'll use that one instead."

Joachim pointed to the smaller loom leaning against the wall next to the window. It consisted of a wooden frame with a pole across the top, another one near the bottom, and one more in the middle, resting on pegs hammered into the frame either side.

"My father taught me to weave standing in front of that, and I've taken great care of it ever since. Look, the warp is still on it. Can you count the threads?"

"Yes father, there are seven white ones alternating with seven black ones. The white ones are attached to the top and bottom bars, but the black ones hang loose."

"Correct! That's how it's supposed to be. When we weave, the white ones stay fixed in place and the black ones are pulled back and forth as we pass the thread between them. But you will learn all of that. For now I want you to go and find seven rough stones as big as your fist. We're going to tie those to the bottom of the black threads."

Saul ran outside and was soon back with seven large stones. His father took one and tied it to the bottom of one of the black threads. Saul helped him with the remaining six stones.

"We will begin the lessons properly tomorrow," his father said. "When your birthday arrives, we'll be able to get you started on your first little rug."

On his birthday, Saul's mother had spun pretty wool for him, ready for weaving. Saul's father stood next to him in front of the loom, teaching him how to weave, just as he had shown him how to make tents. In this way, Saul began to learn his trade as a weaver and tentmaker.

One day when he got home from school, Saul went to the workshop to see his father. Joachim was sitting at the loom with the shuttle in his hand, passing it back and forth. Saul had only just begun to use the large loom, and although he was still quite small and the loom was large, he was beginning to get the hang of it. The smaller loom stood once more against the wall next to the window. The rug Saul had begun on his twelfth birthday now lay on the floor next to his bed, and he had made many more since then.

Saul sat down on a pile of skins and watched his father as he worked. A new tent lay nearby.

"Who is that for?" Saul asked.

"The shepherds in the mountains," his father replied.

"Are they coming to pick it up?"

"No, they aren't able to leave their flocks, so I will have to take it to them. Would you like to come with me?"

"Yes, please. Do the shepherds live up in the mountains then?"

"During the summer they do. There are wonderful pastures up there, as well as lakes and villages. It's quite a climb, but I always enjoy visiting."

Saul's father asked him how school had been and Saul told him about his day. When he had finished, his father asked: "Have you given any more thought to where you would like to go once you have become a scholar of the Law?"

Saul thought about this for a moment.

"I don't know, Father," he said. "My Greek teacher said that I'm still too young to know, but in a few years I might hear a voice that will tell me. Not in a dream but during the day, a voice that tells me what I want to do."

"Did your teacher mean the voice of an angel?" his father asked.

"I don't know, perhaps. In any case, he said that voice is very near, close to your heart. He said that when you hear it, you sense that it already knows what you want, even if you're still unsure. He called it the voice of your *conscience*. He said that you are yourself that voice and, at the same time, it is greater than you are yourself."

Saul's father listened carefully as he made another few passes with his shuttle.

"I am sure your teacher is right," he said, "for he knows a lot. But whatever way that voice shows you, you will have to walk it yourself, and that may be quite a climb too."

They both rose early the next morning to begin their journey into the mountains. They divided up the tent between them. Saul's father carried most of it on his back and gave Saul the groundsheet and the ropes and poles. Then they set off. After they had been climbing for a while, they stopped to rest. Sitting on a large rock by the side of the path, they drank some of the water Saul's father had brought in a leather flask and ate some of the bread and cheese he had wrapped in a cloth. It was near dawn and on the horizon they could see the bright glow of the sun just before it rose.

"Well Saul," his father said, "I think it would be good if you became a rabbi, a teacher. You talk about so many things even your mother and I have never thought about."

"But Father, there is still so much that I don't understand. For example, the rabbi told us about the coming of the Messiah. But what is supposed to happen when the Messiah comes? One rabbi says that everything will be made good, but another predicts that everything will perish in fire and earthquakes."

"Well Saul, my grandmother used to put it like this: she said that when the Messiah comes it will be like the sun." Joachim pointed to where the sun was beginning to rise. "Down there lies Syria, and beyond that lies Persia. After the sun stands high over Persia, it will take its course over Arabia, Israel, Egypt and Crete, and then on to Greece and Rome and Spain, and whatever lands may lie beyond them."

As he spoke, Joachim made a great arc in the air with his hand, rising from the horizon in the east, high up in the sky to the south, and descending in the west. "That is the path the sun will travel today, and that is the path it travels, day in day out, throughout the year, a little lower in the winter, a little higher in the summer. I am no scholar, but I sincerely hope that the Messiah will come in this way, just as my grandmother imagined it. As a light for all the people on earth, one that shines in the east and is seen in the west."

Saul and his father sat in silence together, watching the sun as it rose while they ate their bread and cheese and sipped at their water. Then they gathered their bundles and continued their climb.

II

Saul's time in Tarsus was swiftly coming to an end. One day, when he was fifteen, Dina came to the workshop and put down ten big skeins of the wool that she had spun and dyed a rich red.

"Here they are," she said to Joachim. "It's good wool and the colour won't fade now that it is dry. It will look good on him, he will stand out in a crowd and everyone will see him coming. Don't make the cloak too thin. Jerusalem is high up; you know how cold it can get there."

"Don't worry," said Joachim. "It will keep him warm for many years. When I make a cloak, I make it to last a long time." He picked up the wool and passed it through his hands, feeling the quality.

"Will you make it before Saul leaves? Is the loom ready?"

Joachim nodded. "I always set up the warp ahead of time when there's a job coming in. Now that I have the wool I can make a start on this today. If you hold the first skein for me, I will fill the shuttle with it."

Joachim began work on the cloak after lunch. He liked to sing when he was weaving and all that afternoon his voice could be heard coming from the workshop, carrying above the clatter of the loom as he passed the shuttle back and forth.

A month later, Saul was ready to leave for Jerusalem. He went down to the waterfront accompanied by his parents and his sister. Saul had his bag with him, and his father carried a large pack held together by a belt. Dina walked hand in hand with Esther, who had just turned five. The captain was already looking out for them. He greeted them and took Saul's bag to put in a good spot in the hold.

Dina and Esther unbound the large pack and brought out the cloak Joachim had made for his son. Saul took the cloak, wide-eyed with surprise, and looked it over inside and out.

"Try it on," his mother said.

Saul wrapped the cloak around his shoulders, feeling the reassuring weight and thickness of it.

"It fits him just right," said the captain, full of admiration. "And so nice and thick!"

"Thank you. It's beautiful," Saul said. He could feel a lump forming in his throat, and tears were stinging his eyes.

"Prince Saul," Esther sang. She danced up and down at her mother's side and they all laughed.

The captain stood at the top of the gangplank, waiting for them to say their goodbyes.

"It's time," Dina said.

They wrapped their arms around Saul in a tight and tender embrace.

"Take care, my son," his father said. "Write to us, let us know how you are getting on."

"I will," Saul replied.

"We love you very much," his mother said. "We're so proud of you."

"Thank you," Saul said. "I love you too."

"What about me?" Esther said, tugging on Saul's cloak.

"Yes, I love you too," Saul said, and he knelt down to give his little sister a big hug.

As Saul boarded the ship, the captain put an arm around his shoulder.

"Off on your adventures at last?" he said.

"Yes, Captain."

"Then we'd best be on our way. You've waited long enough."

The captain disappeared to make the final preparations for the journey. Saul went to the stern and as the ship set sail he waved to his parents and his sister. He was excited for this new chapter in his life, but he was still sad to be leaving. He wondered when he would see them again.

3: Arriving in Jerusalem

I

"Hey boy, come and look!"

The captain's booming voice travelled the length of the ship to where Saul was sitting near the stern. Saul walked over to the captain at the bow, standing against the railing.

"See, in front of us is the port of Joppa. It's not the biggest port, but it can still take this ship. Now, look beyond it and tell me what your young eyes see in the distance."

Saul shielded his eyes against the bright afternoon sun and peered out from under his hand.

"I can see a flat, brownish yellow streak, and above it are two bright yellow dots, sparkling in the sun," he said.

"That's the old city wall of Jerusalem, my friend, and the new palace of Herod that sticks out along its western side," the captain said. "If the wind keeps up like this, we'll arrive in port in half an hour. You'd better pack your things and get ready. I trust you're planning on hiring a driver with a donkey. Jerusalem is about thirty miles from the docks."

Saul looked at the captain and smiled.

"I can still walk a fair distance today," he said. "I'll find somewhere to sleep tonight and then continue on in the morning. I'll be in the city by tomorrow evening. You see, Captain, you may have sea legs, but I have *mountain* legs."

Saul clapped his hands on his strong, stout thighs.

"I once hiked all the way to the top of the Taurus Mountains with my father. We delivered a tent to the shepherds who lived up there. When we reached the top, we looked down and saw the River Cydnus like a ribbon of silver shining in the sun. We were so high up we couldn't even pick out our house. That was much harder than the journey ahead of me now. I'm looking forward to it, in fact. I will see Jerusalem getting closer and closer. I can't imagine anything more magnificent. Just think, this is the city of my people, the city of my ancestors: Abraham, Isaac, Jacob, King David himself..."

"I'm afraid those old fellows don't mean much to me," the captain said. "Tell me, are you really going to become a rabbi? Like the ones who read those big books all day long?"

"Yes, I hope so," Saul replied.

"Well, if you become one of those, you can forget your mountain legs," the captain said, and laughed. "Still, I hope you enjoy your walk, and may God go with you."

As they neared the port the captain had work to do. Saul asked him how much he owed him for the voyage.

"Nothing, my boy, nothing at all," he replied, as he made his way to the helmsman at the stern. "Your father took care of everything."

Saul called out after him, "If I should need a boat sometime, will you take me again?"

"As long as you don't become a dried-out bookworm. They don't belong on this ship. They blow overboard with the slightest breeze," the captain said, his loud, booming laughter rolling across the deck from the stern.

II

The rest of Saul's journey proceeded much as he described it to the captain. He took the main road out of Joppa and walked until sundown. When he came to a small town he found a room above an inn where he spent the night. The next morning, he set off again. Always he kept his eyes on Jerusalem, watching the city draw tantalisingly closer as the day wore on. Towards evening, as the light was beginning to fade, Saul came to the top of a rise. To his right were the three gigantic towers of Herod's palace, and on his left was a small hill that looked like a cemetery. A few ancient olive trees grew on its slopes, their trunks grey, half decayed and full of scales, but on the sunny side Saul could see new shoots growing. They reminded him of the tree in his parents' garden where he had so often picked olives. On that tree, too, new shoots had sprung from the grey bark.

"That hill there is Golgotha," said a man standing nearby. "It is the resting place of our ancestors. I always like to see it in the evening light."

Saul looked at it a little longer and then continued on into the city. He entered through the Garden Gate and walked until he had left the palace of Herod behind him. He came to a long low area that stretched from left to right, and on top of the hill beyond it stood two more enormous buildings. The square colossus on the left had to be the Antonia Fortress that the Romans had built, and the massive, rectangular edifice to its right must be the temple, which King Herod had greatly enlarged. The temple had always stood on the hill Moriah, and the Antonia Fortress

had been added to it later on the north side, which meant the Roman soldiers could enter the temple forecourt straight from their fortress.

Saul dropped his pack in astonishment and sat down. It was all so different from the stories his parents and teachers had told him about the kings and the prophets, about David and Solomon, Elijah and Isaiah.

What had the Romans done to beautiful, sacred Jerusalem?

Saul tried to think away those grandiose buildings. Instead, he imagined the modest old temple that King Solomon had built, and behind the Antonia Fortress he pictured the Lion's Gate and the Kidron valley beyond it with its cemeteries. He imagined himself walking through those ancient streets thronging with people, taking in the sights and sounds and smells, the textures and the tastes.

"Yes," he murmured to himself. "That's the way it must have looked. That's the city in which my ancestors once lived."

After a while, Saul got to his feet and picked up his pack. He was looking forward to a good night's sleep after such a long walk. All the more so because he had an important meeting in the morning. He was going to see the chief rabbi to talk about his further schooling.

As the shadows lengthened, Saul went in search of somewhere to spend the night, while in his mind he continued to explore those teeming streets of long ago.

III

"Who are you?"

The chief rabbi, flanked by two rabbis of a lower rank, looked down at Saul with a stern gaze. In his hand he held the letter of introduction Saul had been given by his teacher Athenodorus.

"My name is Saul, although in some places I am known as Paul."

"Who is your father?"

"Joachim of Tarsus. He is a tentmaker and belongs to the order of the Pharisees."

"And what does your mother do?"

"My mother, Dina, takes care of my father, my sister and her own aged parents, as well as helping the poor and the sick in our neighbourhood. She also spins the wool my father needs for his weaving."

"How old are you?"

"Fifteen."

"What languages do you speak?"

"Hebrew, Greek and Latin."

"And what do you expect to learn here?"

"I hope to learn the true meaning of the Jewish laws, to live by those laws faithfully and thus learn to know the Coming One, the Messiah. That seems to me the most wonderful thing there is, and I want to be part of all of that."

The words poured out of Saul in a breathless rush. The chief rabbi looked at him for a moment, then his stern expression softened to a smile.

"I see you are in a great hurry," he said.

Saul blushed. His teachers had often told him that he was too hasty, and that it would be better if he took up his tasks more calmly and finished them more thoroughly.

"Rabbi, my haste is like a racehorse, but I hope to keep a strong hand on the reins."

The other two rabbis smiled and nodded to their leader.

"Far be it from me to hold up one so eager," the chief rabbi said. "You may start whenever you're ready. I have one piece of advice for you: try to attend the lessons of our old rabbi, Gamaliel. There are ordinary rabbis and there are special rabbis. Gamaliel is one of the special ones."

4: Saul's Long Search for the Messiah

I

Saul spent the next ten years studying in Jerusalem. He learned the history of his people and studied their laws, and he worked hard to follow them, just as he had told the chief rabbi he would. He was instructed in all the services and customs in the temple, and he came to understand more deeply the hope and longing of Israel. Every Israelite was looking forward to the coming of the Messiah, their great king. When the Messiah came, everything would change: the old world would pass away and a new, more beautiful one would begin.

Saul, being a good student and keen to think for himself, was full of questions. He asked his teachers and fellow students whether those changes would really happen. Weren't there a lot of beautiful things already in the world, even if it was old? Saul remembered how he had watched the sunrise with his father. When the sun appeared, the darkness, mist and cold had simply evaporated. Saul imagined the coming of the Messiah would be a bit like that. When the Messiah finally appeared, there would be no more darkness anywhere. Saul asked whether Moses and the prophets had said anything about the nature of the world after the Messiah arrived, but even old Gamaliel could not answer those questions. Saul realised he would have to search for the answers himself. When the Messiah came, there would need to be people who were able to recognise him and who could help him.

Saul was filled with the need to find answers to his questions. Then, one day, it occurred to him that the Messiah might already be here. What if they had passed each other in the street? It was agonising for Saul to think that he might not recognise the Messiah when he appeared. The very idea kept him awake at night.

He couldn't let that happen, he told himself. He would have to look harder.

II

It was around this time, as he neared the end of his studies, that Saul heard people talking about a man called John the Baptist. He had appeared from out of the desert claiming that the Kingdom of God was at hand and calling for people to repent. He had begun to baptise people in the River Jordan and a following had grown up around him.

Upon hearing this, Saul went immediately to the River Jordan, where he joined the crowds who were listening to John and who had themselves been baptised by him. In John, Saul saw a true leader, as fiery and as straightforward as himself. He began to wonder if perhaps John the Baptist was the one he had been looking for all this time.

Then, one afternoon, a group of priests came from Jerusalem and challenged John. They demanded to know if he was the Messiah or Elijah or one of the other great prophets. John freely admitted that he wasn't any of these. Instead, he declared that someone far greater than he was coming, and that while he, John, baptised with water, this other would baptise with fire and the Holy Spirit. When he heard this, Saul realised his search for the Messiah was not over.

Three more years passed and Saul continued to search. Then, on the Sunday before Passover, he heard a great commotion in the streets outside his room. He stepped into the street and saw crowds of people streaming through the East Gate, jostling each other as they made their way into the city. They were jubilant and crying out in excitement:

"He is coming! Look, he is coming!"

Saul let himself be carried along by the crowd, but there were so many people he couldn't see what was happening. He heard people shouting that the one they had been waiting for was approaching the gate with his disciples. Saul turned to a man standing next to him.

"Who are they talking about?" he asked.

"Jehosha of Nazareth," the man replied. "The prophet."

Saul thought he had heard the name before. The Greeks called this man Iesos, but many people knew him by his Roman name, Jesus. Saul had overheard some of the priests in the temple talking about him. He was a troublemaker and a blasphemer, and he was from Nazareth of all places! Nothing good could come from Nazareth as everyone knew. It was a quiet village in Galilee, completely unimportant and not really Jewish anyway. It was mostly inhabited by Essenes. In the eyes of the Jewish leaders the Essenes were a strange people. They kept themselves apart from others and you never saw them on important occasions. This Jesus of Nazareth couldn't be the Messiah.

Saul thanked the man and returned to his room to resume his studying.

But five days later the people were once again in the streets because of this Jesus of Nazareth, and Saul later heard from his friends that the man had been put to death. He had been crucified like a criminal, between two other criminals, on Golgotha, the same hill that had been pointed out to Saul the day he arrived in Jerusalem.

It felt, strangely, as though something significant had happened. Saul wondered whether he should have gone out when he'd heard the crowds, but it had been the day before Passover, so he would have had to neglect his religious duties. Saul didn't believe Jesus of Nazareth was the Messiah, but there was something about his death that made him despair of ever finding Israel's great king. And so it was that, after many years of searching and hoping, Saul finally gave up looking.

III

To Saul's surprise, people didn't stop talking about Jesus of Nazareth. Instead, they started saying remarkable things about him. His disciples said that although Jesus had died he had nevertheless risen from the dead. He had conquered death, and not just for himself but for everyone.

More remarkable still, other people were actually *listening* to them. Jesus' disciples were beginning to build a following, and a great many more joined them after Pentecost, fifty days after Passover, when the disciples seemed to be infused with a tireless new energy and a boundless new inspiration. They started calling themselves apostles and went everywhere, telling people who their master was and why they followed him.

Saul saw them in the street engaged in discussion with each other or holding conversations with members of the public. He did not stop to listen to them, as once he had with John the Baptist, and neither did the apostles come to talk to him, which he thought was a little disrespectful. He was a scholar of the Law after all, a member of the order of the Pharisees.

"They are just fishermen, whereas *I* have spent ten years studying the Scriptures," he said to himself. "I am still searching for the truth and yet these simple people act as if they possess the truth already."

Saul felt sure of himself, yet the attitude of the disciples puzzled him greatly. He noticed that more people were coming to them all the time.

In the years that followed, the new community continued to grow. The apostles looked after all those who came to them, preparing meals for their communal services and caring for their sick and elderly.

Saul was also busy through that time. He rose to become a leader of his people. He was given the task of ensuring that the Jewish laws were precisely followed. He was well known, and his mastery of three languages meant that he was able to speak with almost everyone.

He continued to hear about the apostles and their growing congregation, or the People of the Way of Jesus as they liked to call themselves, but he dismissed them as nothing more than a nuisance. Groups of people who believed in strange new things were always springing up around

Jerusalem, but they never lasted long. People quickly lost interest and moved on to the next thing. Saul, pondering on the new band of believers, decided it would be the same for them.

Three years after the crucifixion of Jesus of Nazareth, Saul was in a synagogue in Jerusalem when a leader of the People of the Way of Jesus stood up to speak. His name was Stephen. He was Greek and he had been appointed by the apostles to be a deacon of their community. In front of the people in the synagogue, Stephen accused the Jews of treason and rebelliousness against their real leaders.

Upon hearing this, the Jews erupted in anger. They seized Stephen and dragged him out of the synagogue. They took him to the Sanhedrin, the Supreme Council of the Israelites, and demanded that he explain himself before these high functionaries.

Stephen said: "I am standing in the place where Jesus also stood when he was condemned by you three years ago. Jesus kept his silence then, but today I will tell you the truth. And that truth is that throughout our history almost all the great leaders of the Jewish people were reviled and betrayed by their own people. Abraham had to escape from Mesopotamia; Jacob had to flee because of his brother Esau; Moses was threatened by his own people in the desert, and David, our greatest king, had to run because he was attacked by the army of his own son Absalom. But the greatest crime was committed here, by you, when you condemned Jesus, our greatest prophet, and had him crucified outside the city walls."

When the members of the Supreme Council heard this they gnashed their teeth in rage. They made a sign to

Saul who commanded the guards to seize Stephen. They dragged him out through the city gate to the place where they stoned criminals, an amphitheatre carved out of the surrounding rock. They threw him down in the middle. Already a crowd was beginning to gather. Saul stood at the entrance, where people had put their cloaks to keep them out of the way during the stoning.

Saul's gaze was irresistibly drawn to Stephen. He seemed to be bathed in light, as though an angel stood next to him to give him strength and support in his final moments.

With the first stone, Stephen fell to the ground. He looked up and cried:

"Jesus, Lord, receive my spirit!"

As he looked around at his executioners, his eyes settled on Saul.

With an effort, Stephen said, "Lord, do not hold this sin against them." Then he collapsed and died.

Saul should have felt satisfied, the Law had been upheld, justice had been served. But instead he was deeply troubled. In Stephen's eyes he had seen no trace of fear or pain or hatred. They had shone with a heavenly radiance and were looking into the distance at something invisible, something Saul could not see.

It weighed on Saul's mind for the rest of the day, and when he was alone in his room that evening it came back to him with great force. In his mind's eye, he pictured Stephen, this man who had shown no trace of fear or anger, who was concerned not for himself and his own ordeal, but for those killing him. It was as though he could see that the day would come when they would all be judged for this terrible murder. In Stephen's eyes Saul had seen not accusation, but love.

Saul asked himself why he had gone along with the senseless wave of excitement that had led to Stephen's death. It had not felt like justice, so why had he assisted the guards and stood with the crowd?

Saul had agreed with the Supreme Council's judgement, he agreed that Stephen's teachings were wrong. But putting the Greek man to death also felt wrong. Saul had been struck by a kind of numbness during the stoning. He had been there, but he had not been fully present somehow.

Amid these questions, Saul began to wonder if perhaps he had heard the voice of his own heart, what his teachers back home had called conscience.

But Saul was tenacious as well as strong. He did not easily let go of the things he believed in, even if he had begun to question them. The next morning he remembered how deeply Stephen had insulted him and the other scholars of the Law, and he pushed aside his compassion for the man. He made the decision there and then to persecute these obstinate People of the Way of Jesus, and deal with them just as the Supreme Council had with Stephen.

He went to the high priests and asked them to give him the power to persecute the People of the Way of Jesus, wherever they might be. Many of the apostles and their followers had already left the city out of fear for their lives. Saul's request was granted. He was ordered to find these people who had gone astray, take them prisoner and bring them back to Jerusalem to face a fate like Stephen's.

Filled with a renewed zeal, and convinced that this was his mission, Saul gathered his companions and left Jerusalem, heading north towards Damascus.

5: Damascus

I

It was a long and arduous journey. Saul and his companions travelled on foot through bare country, the sun beating mercilessly down on them. Saul struggled with sleep. Whenever he closed his eyes, he was visited by terrible dreams. He heard the indignant voices of his teachers who said that Jesus came from Galilee and no real prophet of Israel could ever come from there. He saw Stephen at his trial before the Supreme Council, claiming Jesus had been Israel's *greatest* prophet and blaming the Jewish rabbis for his death, and he dreamt of Stephen at his stoning, asking God to forgive his killers.

During the day, Saul kept returning to the same questions that had been troubling his mind. Was it right to execute a person just for saying what they honestly believed? Should they not be allowed to express their most deeply held convictions? And how could people believe in something that the rabbis agreed was wrong?

After eight restless days and sleepless nights, Saul and his companions finally reached an oasis just outside the city of Damascus. Tall palm trees with their high crowns of leaves grew alongside gnarled olive trees and laurel bushes with their hard fruits, as well as fragrant myrtle, oleanders, and wide-reaching oaks. Streams ran between the trees and there were ponds where travellers could quench their thirst. It was a beautiful sight after the hard, rocky countryside, and the shade was a welcome relief from the heat.

While his companions refreshed themselves eating and drinking, Saul stood in a clearing. He breathed the fragrant air and felt the gentle breeze against his skin. The stress and strain that had burdened him so heavily suddenly lifted and for a moment he felt strangely carefree. A light shone around him. At first Saul thought it was the sun standing overhead at midday, and he stepped back into the shade. But the light grew brighter, more intense, until Saul was overwhelmed by it and sank to the ground. Then he heard a voice say:

"Saul, Saul, why do you persecute me?"

The voice seemed to sound from the farthest reaches of heaven even as it spoke in the innermost depths of Saul's heart. Whoever was speaking knew him inside and out. Saul was filled with fear and wonder and his heart trembled as he felt a powerful presence surrounding him.

"Who are you, Lord?" he stammered.

"I am Jesus, the one you are persecuting!"

When Saul realised who was speaking, all his ambition and self-righteous certainty melted away. He longed to know what this voice wanted from him.

"What do you want me to do, Lord?"

"Get up and go into the city. There you will be told what you are to do."

As Saul lay on the ground, his companions gathered around him. They had also heard the voice, but they couldn't see where it was coming from or who was

speaking. Their leader seemed to be talking to someone invisible. They were stunned and a little afraid.

Then Saul sat up. He stretched out his hands as if groping for something and called out. His companions answered, but from the frightened and bewildered look on Saul's face it was clear he could not see them. He was blind.

Saul's companions helped him to his feet and, taking him by the hand, led him into the city of Damascus.

II

The People of the Way of Jesus who had fled Jerusalem were living in Damascus, along with a number of others there who also followed Jesus. Among them was a man called Ananias. One day, Jesus appeared to Ananias in a vision.

"Ananias, go to the house of Judas on Straight Street. There you will find a man called Saul of Tarsus, who came here from Jerusalem. He cannot see and he has not eaten or drunk anything for three days. Go to him, lay your hands on him and baptise him, and through you I will heal him. Saul has been praying, he has seen that you will come to him."

Ananias said, "But Lord, isn't this the same man who has persecuted your people in Jerusalem?"

"It is," came the answer, "but I have chosen him to serve me and to go before me among the Gentiles, among all those who are not Jewish. This have I told him."

So Ananias went to the house of Judas on Straight Street where he found Saul waiting for him. He told Saul what he had heard. Ananias placed his hands on Saul, blessed him and baptised him. In that moment Saul's sight was restored and he saw the light streaming in through the windows. But he also received the gift of an even greater light, one that shone within him and showed him all the roads he would travel in service to his Lord. It was the light of the Holy Spirit and, after his baptism and the laying on of hands, it would never leave him in all the years to come.

III

Saul now burned with enthusiasm to tell everyone in Damascus what had happened to him. His words were like fire. At first, people were alarmed. A few who belonged to the People of the Way of Jesus began to trust him, but most remained suspicious. The Jews also kept reminding him – and everyone else – that he had persecuted the People of the Way of Jesus, yet now here he was spreading their lies. It made them angry and they made plans to chase Saul away or even kill him. Saul was so eager to share what he had experienced that he did not realise people were plotting against him. In the end, Saul was warned by his host, Judas, and by Ananias. He understood then that he had to leave.

That same night Saul slipped out of the city and hid in the oasis. As he lay looking up at the moon, he recalled the morning long ago when he had got up early with his father to take the tent to the shepherds in the mountains. They had stopped to rest for a while and watch the sun as it rose. His father had mentioned the different countries the sun would pass over as it continued to rise.

Down there lies Syria, and beyond that lies Persia. After the sun stands high over Persia, it will take its course over Arabia, Israel, Egypt, and Crete.

Saul murmured to himself, "Arabia."

Moses had spent a long time in Arabia.

Saul recalled the stories about the prophet leading his people out of bondage in Egypt: their great exodus and perilous journey through the Red Sea pursued by the Egyptians. After that they had wandered in the desert for forty years. It was there that Moses had climbed Mount Sinai and received the Law that governed Jewish life, but the longest part of that time had been spent in the oasis of Kadesh. A friendly people called the Nabateans lived there now; they had their capital in Petra.

Towards morning, Saul knew he wanted to go to Arabia. He had been shown a new way. He wanted to investigate everything about the Law again, and in this very special place the Nabateans would give him the peace he needed to read and reflect.

IV

No sooner had the cock begun crowing than Saul was up and on his way. He had barely slept all night. But this time he was not tormented by dreams of the past, rather he was filled with excitement at what lay ahead of him.

In Sidon, on the coast, Saul found a captain of a ship who let him come aboard. After a two-day voyage along the coast of Palestine, Saul came ashore in the port of Arish. From there he walked south into the desert, leaving Israel behind. After a few days he came to an oasis. In the distance he saw a mountain whose high peak was obscured by cloud.

"That must be where it happened," Saul said. "That must be where Moses climbed up to receive the Law from his God twelve hundred years ago."

Saul learned from other travellers that he had indeed arrived at the oasis of Kadesh, where the Israelites had spent most of their time in the desert. But God's voice no longer sounded from the clouds that hid the top of the mountain. Instead, Saul came to know another voice. It was a still, small voice, that spoke only when Saul was silent and at rest within himself. Saul would ask that voice a question and wait patiently for a reply. Then, between the night and the day, between darkness and light, the voice would answer. In the months that followed it became more and more familiar, but what was most curious about the voice was that when it spoke, Saul knew instinctively that it spoke the truth. It was if he had known all along what he was being told and the voice was simply reminding him.

One day, Saul remembered what his first teacher in Tarsus had told him: each of us can hear a voice that is very close to our heart and that knows what we need. Saul's teacher had called it the voice of conscience. He had said that the voice was each person's truest self, and yet, in some mysterious way, it was far greater than they were. It was the voice of a higher power.

V

Saul stayed near Kadesh for almost three years. Twelve hundred years earlier, in the same place, his people had received the Ten Commandments from Moses. Now Saul learned to listen to the voice of his heart. He learned to understand it better and have more confidence in it. Every time he heard that voice he knew better who it was that was speaking, for it was the same voice he had heard in the oasis outside Damascus. After Saul had listened to this voice for three years he knew that the time had come when the Law of Moses had lost its power. Something new had taken its place, something he had to proclaim to people.

"But when, Lord?" Saul asked, full of impatience.

"First, go back to Damascus," came the answer, "and wait there until I tell you what will happen next."

Saul went to the port of Rafia, where he searched for days for a ship to take him back to Sidon. Then, one day, he saw a ship coming in that looked surprisingly familiar.

Where had he seen it before?

Suddenly, Saul remembered a voice from long ago.

As long as you don't become a dried-out bookworm. They don't belong on this ship. They blow overboard with the slightest breeze.

It was sixteen years since he heard those words on that ship. Could it really be the same ship and the same captain?

Saul waited until the cargo had been unloaded and the new cargo had been stowed, then he took another look at the captain who stood giving orders by the gangplank. He was a little slower perhaps, his hair greyer, his face more weathered and lined, but Saul was certain it was the same man.

The captain noticed Saul looking at him. "Can I help you?"

"I hope so. I'm looking for a ship to take me to Sidon."

"And who are you?"

Saul smiled. "Whoever I am, sir, I am certainly no bookworm."

The captain lifted his hand to shield his eyes from the sun as he peered more closely at Saul. A broad smile spread across his face and he let out a loud burst of laughter.

"Well, we'll just have to see about that," he said. "You'd better come aboard."

The captain gripped Saul by the shoulders with both hands.

"Look at you, you've grown into a man as big as this old sea-dog. Here, sit down and tell me how you've been."

"Captain, I have done what you feared I would. I spent ten years with my nose in books, studying, but after that I learned so much more from people. I have lived for the last three years in this wonderful country where my people once received its laws, but now it's time for me to return. I need to get to Sidon urgently; I am expected in Damascus very soon."

"You're in luck," the captain said. "I have cargo bound for Tyre and Sidon, and room for you too. But autumn is coming, when we get fierce winds. So, my learned gentleman, are you ready for an old-fashioned storm?"

"I'm familiar with storms of all sorts and sizes, and those that are coming now won't be the last either. Take me with you. I don't blow overboard so easily."

"That's what I like to hear," the captain said. "Bring your things and I'll show you to your berth. We sail at sunrise tomorrow."

VI

In Straight Street, Judas and his wife often spoke about Saul. So when he suddenly appeared after three years they sprang up and embraced him with tears of joy. They had a lot to tell each other. Judas and his wife talked about the People of the Way of Jesus, and Saul told of his time in the desert at the oasis of Kadesh.

"Why would you ever want to leave such a remarkable place?" they asked.

"Because of what happened to me at the oasis here," Saul replied. "I am not going back to Kadesh."

"How long do you intend to stay?" Judas asked.

"I don't know yet if this is where I'm meant to be."

The next morning Saul went to see Ananias and the others he knew from his previous stay in Damascus. He visited and talked to people throughout the city, and everywhere he went he spoke about the new laws that had replaced the old ones. Laws that were not written on tablets of stone this time but inscribed in human hearts.

The Greeks and the pagans were eager to hear this and wanted him to talk more about it, but the Jews still did not trust him.

"Aren't you a Pharisee?" they said. "That's what you said you were the last time you were here. But the things you are saying now we have never heard from any Pharisee."

Saul replied, "Our holy Scripture says that one day the Messiah will come. I tell you now that this has happened. Jesus of Nazareth was the Messiah. He was crucified and died in Jerusalem, but his heavenly Father raised him from the dead and gave him a new life."

"How can you possibly know that?" the Jews asked.

"Three years ago, outside this very city, he appeared to me himself and told me."

The Jews became angry. "You don't expect us to believe such fairy tales do you? We know what our Scriptures say, and we don't accept your twisted version! Go tell your stories to others. Get out of here and don't come back!"

Saul tried again to explain, but his friends intervened at that point and took him back to the house of Judas.

That night they returned with a big basket and a rope and took him to a house built into the city wall.

"Our Jewish neighbours are feeling threatened, and they want to kill you," they said. "For now you must go somewhere else, but know that we still trust you and will always help you in the future."

So, in the middle of the night, Saul squeezed into the basket and was lowered from a little window down the outside of the wall. At the bottom, he wiggled out and hurried to the oasis, where he found the place he had hidden himself three years before. He saw, too, the place where that heavenly light had overwhelmed him and he had fallen to the ground, where the voice of the Risen One had spoken to him, telling him things that even now he did not fully comprehend. No wonder others struggled to understand him when he had such difficulty expressing his message himself. He understood their urge to kill him. After all, hadn't he been like them once?

For now at least, he was safe. Saul sat down against a tree, and because he was so tired he fell immediately asleep.

VII

When Saul woke early in the morning, he lay contemplating the events of the past few days. Why had he spoken so soon about what had happened to him here in the oasis? He had caught those good people completely off guard, just as he had done three years ago. Had he once again been too hasty? Perhaps. But everything he had experienced was so shockingly new that he wanted to share it with everyone!

With a groan Saul sat up.

He considered his rash, impatient behaviour. He realised he had never made contact with the other followers of Jesus, with the disciples who had known Jesus in earthly life. Saul now saw his lack of respect for the apostles Peter, James and John, and for everything they must have experienced. He remembered how he had spoken with contempt of the Essenes and had avoided their house by King David's grave. A woman called Mary lived there with her son John, who was called by his surname Mark. The apostles were frequent visitors, and Stephen, as deacon of their community, had used that house as a base for his activity. Many of those people had frequently been with Jesus.

When Saul realised all of this he was greatly ashamed for the way he had behaved, and he decided to visit that house

THE REMARKABLE STORY OF PAUL THE APOSTLE

first of all. He wanted to get to know the people there, to hear about their experiences, and learn what Jesus had commanded them to do.

Saul got to his feet. The first light of day glowed in the east and, behind him, Damascus was slowly coming to life. He turned towards the mountains in the distance and started walking south.

6: Saul Returns to Jerusalem

I

After eight days, Saul reached the heights of the city of Gibeon and from there he could see Jerusalem. He knew it would take him another two hours to reach the nearest city gate, which he could just make out in the distance. It was the Essene Gate. Saul sat down. Seeing it again brought back memories of Stephen's stoning that were so intense he had to force himself to think of something else.

He wondered to whom he would go when he first entered the city. Certainly not to his old study companions, they did not trust him any more, and not to the circle of the twelve apostles either, they knew him only as the man who had gone to Damascus to persecute the People of the Way of Jesus. Everyone in Jerusalem probably hated and feared him.

Then, Saul remembered his friend Barnabas, who belonged to the Levites, the Jewish tribe of temple servants. Saul had studied with him in Jerusalem and he had heard that Barnabas had joined the People of the Way. Barnabas had a sister called Mary, the same Mary who lived in the house of the Essenes with her son, John Mark. Barnabas had lived on the island of Cyprus for a long time and spoke Greek, just like Saul.

Yes, Barnabas was an open-minded person, he would give Saul a fair hearing and would not reject his old friend out of hand. With all his fragile hope resting on this one trustworthy person, Saul got to his feet and walked the last stretch of his journey, returning to the city that now seemed incredibly important in his journey.

II

As he neared the city gate, Saul came to the amphitheatre where criminals were stoned. He stood motionless for a moment, this time allowing the powerful rush of memories to wash over him.

"Ah, Stephen," he said to himself. "I wish you were still here. If you were, I would gladly stand side by side with you."

Saul blinked away tears and carried on.

He went directly to the house of the Essenes in search of Barnabas. Mary, Barnabas's sister, opened the door to Saul. She was surprised at first, but she let him in. She found him a place to sit, brought him food and drink, and sat down with him. A few moments later the door opened again and a big, broad-shouldered man appeared. Mary went to the kitchen to get more food and drink as the man crossed the room to where Saul was sitting.

"Saul, I have heard so much about you," he said. "I have thought of you and dreamt of you, and now here you are, sitting in my sister's house!"

He opened his arms and embraced Saul.

When Mary saw this she called out to her son, John Mark. They drew their chairs together around Saul's table. They had much to tell each other. Mary mentioned one event after another that had taken place at her house, and afterwards Barnabas spoke about Jesus' disciples Peter, James, John, and the others. John Mark told him of the time he had seen Roman soldiers try to seize Jesus, but for some reason they had not been able to lay their hands on him. He had slipped through their fingers.

Saul explained what had happened to him, though he struggled sometimes to find the words to describe it all. He told them he urgently wanted to speak with the People of the Way of Jesus in Jerusalem.

"I have a lot to learn, and I have many questions," he said. "And I have my own story to tell too."

III

The next day Barnabas took Saul to see Simon Peter.

"Here is a man who knows Jerusalem better than any of us," Barnabas said to Peter. "He studied here for ten years and is a scholar of the Law. He speaks Hebrew, and he is fluent in Greek and Latin. He doesn't come from the provinces as most of us do, but grew up in Tarsus, the capital of the East-Roman Empire. The rest I will let him tell you himself."

Peter welcomed Saul and took him to meet the other apostles. Saul had long conversations with them, especially with John and James, the brother of Jesus. He listened to their stories about Jesus and everything they had experienced alongside him, eager to hear every detail. Then he told the apostles his own story, about his own encounter with Jesus in the oasis outside Damascus, and the task he had received there. The apostles listened to Saul as keenly as he had to them, and they were filled with surprise and wonder.

Peter then took Saul to see the places in Jerusalem where they had experienced remarkable things with Jesus. He showed Saul the pool of Bethesda, where a man had been healed of his paralysis after thirty-eight years. He also showed Saul the upper room in Mary's house where the apostles had gathered so often and where they had experienced the Last Supper and the miracle of Pentecost.

When he heard these stories and saw these places, a deep, thoughtful mood came over Saul.

"In all those years I was never aware of any of this," he said. "I had set myself the task of learning all I could about the Messiah so that one day, when he came, I would recognise him, and yet here he was under my nose the whole time and I didn't even know."

In the days that followed, Saul and the apostles got to know each other and slowly came to trust each other.

Saul's encounter with his former study companions, however, did not go as well.

These men were now the leaders of the Jewish people and taught what was written in the Jewish Law. They listened to Saul explain how the old Law had come to an end, replaced by a new one that spoke of mercy and love. The Jewish leaders voiced one objection after another, but when they saw that Saul had an answer for each one they became angry. It wasn't long before they began forming plans to get rid of him.

Just as in Damascus, Saul's life was once again in danger.

7: Saul Becomes Paul

I

It was Barnabas who intervened in the end. He and the apostles agreed that Saul should take a break for a while, and so Barnabas went with him to Joppe where Saul could get a ship to Tarsus.

"Are you sending me home?" Saul said, discouraged and angry. "I suppose it is time I went back to see my parents. It's been so long since I left them, I don't even know how they are. But Barnabas, I still believe I have been given a task. How can I do my work in Tarsus?"

"Talk to people. Tell whoever will listen what has happened to you," Barnabas said. "The Jews speak Hebrew but everyone else speaks Greek. Think of all the people you can reach with that language. Not only is it spoken in Greece and throughout its islands, but all over Asia Minor. Don't you think those people would like to know that the Messiah has come to earth? And who better to tell them than someone who can speak like you? Whenever I hear you speak, my ears instantly perk up."

Barnabas waited for Saul to reply, but Saul was lost in thought. In his mind he saw the great Greek cities of Athens, Corinth and Thessalonica, and over in Asia Minor he saw Ephesus and Troas, as well as the Celtic province of Galatia. It was such a large stretch of land, so rich in history and culture that Saul was overwhelmed by it.

"You are very quiet," said Barnabas after a while.

Saul sighed. "I see so much before me."

"That's a good thing, isn't it?" asked Barnabas.

"Yes, a very good thing. But why must I go to Tarsus first?"

"The Jews in Israel may know the power of their words," Barnabas said, "but I don't believe they have spent much time thinking about them. They may be filled with the richness and wonder of their own language, but are they able to have any new thoughts of their own? The Greeks on the other hand are very different. They think more freely, they are less bound by rules and tradition, and they have many new ideas. I know this to be true because I grew up among Greeks on Cyprus, and you know it because you grew up among them in Tarsus. That is why you must go there first."

The road began to rise beneath their feet, getting steeper as they climbed the hill. When they reached the top they paused for a moment to catch their breath and looked out over the harbour and the deep blue waters of the Mediterranean.

"You're right," Saul said. "The Greek language has thoughts that take flight like birds on the wing. They soar far and wide and you can see clearly in all directions. My teachers in Tarsus always said that."

They carried on walking. Barnabas saw that Saul's pace had quickened and there was a spring in his step.

"Saul, slow down, I can't keep up with you," Barnabas said, breathless. "There is one more thing I want to say to you."

"And what is that?"

"The Greeks have a story about how humans got fire. Originally, only their gods had fire. Zeus knew very well not to give it away, because first you have to know how to work with it. But that proud god Prometheus had different ideas. He took the dry stalk of a big fennel and held it against the chariot of the sun as it passed by. The stalk caught fire and Prometheus took this down to Earth and gave it to human beings. It wasn't long before there was fire everywhere on Earth. Zeus was angry and punished Prometheus for his disobedience. He told Hephaistos, the blacksmith of the gods, to chain him to a rock in the Caucasus mountains. Prometheus hung there for a long time until Heracles finally freed him. But the damage was already done, people had been given fire."

"What exactly are you trying to tell me, Barnabas?"

"Fire left to burn causes a great deal of damage, but there is nothing better than a controlled fire. It provides warmth and can preserve life. You must learn to control your own inner fire and use it to do good. Don't let it get out of hand and burn those around you.

"Learn to delve more deeply into the Greek language. It is a language that has been made rich by great artists and wise men. You know their names already: Plato, Aristotle, Socrates, Euripides. You must familiarise yourself with those riches in order to reach the people with your words. You can't do that with Hebrew or Latin. You must become so fluent in Greek that you can say exactly what you want to say. Do that and your words will be like music in their ears!

"Now, hurry down to the harbour. There are ships coming in. Maybe one of them can take you to Tarsus.

I wish you a safe journey, Saul, and may God bless you on your mission. I am sure we will see each other again one day."

II

And so Saul returned to Tarsus. As the city came into view, he realised it had been seventeen years since he had left. In all that time he had seen only one person from here – his sister, Esther. She had moved to Jerusalem with her husband, and they had had a son there. He had been to visit her and asked her how their parents were. Esther said they were well and keeping busy.

When the ship docked, Saul went straight to his parents' house. His mother and father were overjoyed to see him, and they spent the rest of the day talking about everything that had happened since they had last seen each other.

"Have you come to stay?" they asked.

"For a while, yes," said Saul. "I have also come to see my old teachers. I may be a fully qualified rabbi and know the holy Scriptures by heart, but I've realised there is so much more to them. I wish to learn more about Greek culture. I may have learned ordinary, everyday Greek when I was at school, but I know very little about where it came from. I want to immerse myself in Greek language and history."

"I'm sure your teachers will be glad to see you again," his father said.

"You know you have two names, don't you?" his mother said. "Saul is your Jewish name, after the first king of Israel who came from the tribe of Benjamin, as do we. But in Greek your name is Paulos, which the Romans turned into Paulus. If you wish to immerse yourself in the Greek world, why not call yourself Paul?"

Saul thought about this for a moment.

"Paul," he said, trying out the name as once he had tried out his sister's name to see how it would fit. He smiled. "Yes. The name means 'small' or 'humble'. That is good, for that is what I want to be from now on. As a humble student I wish to learn what the Greek language and history have to teach me. After that, I intend to travel a lot, especially to the west. A more modern-sounding name might help me among the Romans. Paul is good. I hope you can get used to it. In the meantime, I must also make a living. Can I work for you, father?"

"Indeed," replied Joachim. "I am receiving more orders than I can handle. You can start tomorrow."

III

The next day Paul went to the well in the marketplace to fetch water. As he was standing in line with his bucket he felt a hand on his shoulder and heard a voice say:

"Saul? Is that you?"

Paul turned around. The man standing in front of him was about the same age as Paul and there was something vaguely familiar about him.

"Kyrill! My old friend!" Paul cried and embraced him. "It's so good to see you again."

The two men stood in line and filled their buckets together. As they were walking away from the well, Kyrill said: "My wife is waiting for me at home, but I want to hear all about what has happened to you, you've been gone such a long time. Come and have dinner with us this evening, you can meet my wife and tell us everything."

That evening was a very happy one with plenty of food and wine. Paul told Kyrill and his wife about his time in Jerusalem and the change that had come over him in the oasis outside Damascus. But he was careful not to get carried away, remembering what Barnabas had told him about controlling his inner fire.

"And what brings you back here after all this time?" Kyrill asked.

"A number of things," Paul said. "Family for one. It's been a long time since I saw my father and mother. But I also have a desire to learn more about Greek language and culture."

Kyrill laughed when he heard this.

"Believe it or not, I'm a teacher of Greek literature at the temple school here in Tarsus."

"Then you must teach me," Paul said, without hesitation. "Let me be one of your students."

"You? A student?" Kyrill laughed again. "But you're a rabbi, a scholar of the Law."

"Yes, that is what I am," Paul said. "But I still have many questions. For Jews, Jerusalem is where we go to uncover the secrets of the past. For the Greeks it is Eleusis near Athens or Ephesus over in Smyrna. I know nothing of either place. I wish to learn as much as I can."

"In that case you are very welcome to join my class," Kyrill said.

And with the last of the wine they celebrated Paul becoming a student once more.

So the learned rabbi Saul became the student Paul. For

one year he wrote down everything his friend and teacher told him.

Kyrill told his students about the demigod Heracles – known as Hercules to the Romans – and how he performed twelve superhuman labours for King Eurystheus. During the last of his ordeals, Heracles descended into Hades to capture the three-headed dog who guarded the gates of the underworld. But even though Heracles succeeded in this task, he was unable to free a single soul from the darkness of that terrible place. On another occasion, Kyrill told them the story of the hero Odysseus. He, too, had gone to the entrance of the underworld and there he had seen the shades of the dead, including that of his own mother. They all complained about the darkness that reigned there, but Odysseus could not enter to help them. He could not save his poor mother.

Finally, Kyrill told them the story of Persephone, the daughter of the heavenly father Zeus and the earth mother Demeter. Persephone had ended up in the underworld after being abducted by the ruler of Hades himself. Demeter was desperate and searched for someone who could free her daughter. She found a young man called Triptolemos, and even though she made him invulnerable, he still could not bring Persephone back. Even the god Dionysus tried to free her, but he was torn apart by the giants known as the Titans.

"And yet," Kyrill said, "the myth says that a new Dionysus will come. He will be much stronger than the first one and will have the power to rescue Persephone from Hades. Unfortunately, I cannot tell you what will happen after that, as the myth does not say. The new Dionysus had not come at that point."

With the telling of that last story a year had passed since Paul had started his studies. He went to his friend to thank him.

"I have learned such a great deal from you," Paul said.

"I'm glad to hear it," Kyrill said. "You're most welcome."

"And I think I have an ending for the last story you told."

Kyrill's face brightened. "Is that so? Then I would love to hear it."

Paul told Kyrill about his time in Jerusalem and how he had studied the books of his ancestors to learn as much as he could about the Messiah: that mighty figure who was to deliver human beings from all suffering and adversity, even from the power of death itself. He told him about the People of the Way of Jesus and how they proclaimed that a simple carpenter from Nazareth called Jesus was in fact the Messiah. He had been crucified and, so they said, raised from the dead. Paul described how hearing this had filled him with fury, and he was determined to wipe out this heresy.

"For that reason I went to Damascus," he said. "But when I reached the oasis outside the city, I was struck by a light many times brighter than the sun. It completely overwhelmed me, and yet for all its power it was also gentle and comforting. All the rage and the hatred I felt for the people I was persecuting melted away in that moment. Then I saw that this light came from a single human being, and this human being told me that he was Jesus of Nazareth who had died and been raised from the dead. He did not have a regular body, of the kind you and I have as we sit here talking. His body was made entirely of light. He gave me the task to go into the world and tell people that death no longer has any power over them. He has conquered death and opened up the way to a higher life in and through him."

"You mean you actually *saw* that he had returned from the underworld, from the realm of the dead?" Kyrill asked, awestruck.

"Yes," Paul said. "And that is why I came back to Tarsus to understand it better. And now, after listening to the stories you've told, I think Jesus has to be the new Dionysus the Greeks are expecting."

Kyrill was silent for a long time.

"That is a lot to take in," he said. "I would like to hear more from you, but I need time to think about what you've said. Come back next week. I will be *your* student and you can be my teacher. I'm sure I will have many questions for you."

IV

When Paul returned the following week, he and Kyrill sat outside under the laurel trees. Paul told him everything that he had experienced since that afternoon in the oasis outside Damascus. Then Kyrill asked his questions. They talked for such a long time that it soon began to get dark, and servants lit torches around them.

"Who or what is this Jesus?" Kyrill asked. "Is he an idea, a thought? Thoughts come and go, and they may be stronger or weaker. Sometimes you really have to look for them, and at other times they force themselves upon you. Is this Jesus an idea?"

"No, he's a human being," Paul replied. "But he can enliven our thinking through the power of his own thoughts. It's a bit like you with your students. When you told us about Heracles, Odysseus, Persephone and Hades, we were able to think along with you. So it is with Jesus Christ, but to a much greater degree. His thoughts are living thoughts, they have the power of eternal life, and when we learn to think through him and in him, we share in this eternal life."

"But how is such a thing possible?"

"Do you remember our great teacher Athenodorus?'

"Certainly I do."

"Do you remember what he told us about our conscience? He said that when we hear our conscience, it is the voice of our angel speaking in our heart, and in that way we come to know something together with our angel. It is the same with Christ. We can know something through him and in him if we are willing to listen, and that too is what we call our conscience."

Kyrill thought about this for some time.

"But if Christ thinks with us he must be alive, for nothing dead can think."

"Correct," Paul said.

"Then this Christ must indeed be the new Dionysus," Kyrill said. "The one who has the strength to break the power of Hades."

8: The First Christians

I

Three years passed. During that time more and more People of the Way of Jesus left Jerusalem, fleeing persecution. They travelled to Phoenicia and Cyprus and to Antioch in Syria to the north where they found each other again. They continued to spread the message about Jesus of Nazareth, but at first only among other Jews.

In Antioch, however, there was a large number of Greek-speaking people from Cyprus and Cyrene. They were eager to share the good news and spoke to any and all who would listen, be they Gentile or Jew, Greek or Roman, for Antioch was a busy, bustling city with people from all over the place. If Jesus came for the whole world, these people said, why should membership of the People of the Way of Jesus be limited only to Jews? Surely, it was open to everyone. As a result of this, many people who were not Jews abandoned their old ways and joined this new community of followers. They lived together, worked together, ate together. They held all things in common and there were no divisions among them.

When the apostles in Jerusalem heard about this they became concerned. In Jerusalem the People of the Way had Peter, James and John to teach them and explain things to them, but in Antioch they had no one who thoroughly understood this. In their boundless enthusiasm for their new faith, they could easily go astray. The apostles decided to send Barnabas to Antioch to investigate matters. Barnabas knew the Way and knew both the Jews and the Greeks. He would be able to help the people there.

Barnabas went to Antioch as instructed and there he found a community of followers all faithfully observing the message of Jesus. It made him glad to see this. When he had been there two years he realised he would need more help. He was extremely busy these days and more and more people came to him with questions. He did his best to answer them according to his own understanding, but Barnabas felt the people here needed a proper teacher. Someone who not only shared their passion and enthusiasm for the good news, but who could also connect it with what had gone before, with the whole history of the Jewish people and the traditions of the holy Scriptures. Someone who could give their faith a firm foundation. Barnabas spent many sleepless nights wondering who this could be. Then he remembered his friend Saul, who was now called Paul.

Yes, he would be perfect!

Barnabas didn't sleep that night either, but this time it was because he was excited. He was eager to see Paul again and hoped to convince him to come to Antioch.

II

Barnabas left for Tarsus the next day. He wondered how easy it would be to find Paul in such a big city, but as soon as he started asking after him, he discovered that people knew Paul well. Barnabas eventually found Paul in his father's tent-making workshop. Paul was delighted to see him again.

"What brings you here?" he asked.

Barnabas told him about the community in Antioch and how they had fled persecution in Jerusalem. They were free, but there were now so many of them that Barnabas needed help.

"They need a teacher," Barnabas said. "Someone who can answer their questions and who knows in his heart what they are looking for. I can think of no one better than you."

Paul agreed to accompany Barnabas to Antioch. The next day they boarded a ship that took them to Seleucia and from there they took the road, reaching the city of Antioch later that day. The city lay spread out before them, cradled in the curve of the River Orontes, which sprang from the mountains far off in the distance and flowed southeast towards the Mediterranean. Paul was deeply impressed; he had never before seen a city like that. He saw the densely packed streets in the centre and the beautiful villas built into the sides of the hills around it. But what surprised him most was a big white cross that divided the city into four parts.

"What is that?" he asked.

"Those are the columned streets," Barnabas replied. "Each of them has four rows of columns that divide the street into three lanes: the middle one for carts, the outer ones for pedestrians. To the left and right you can see shops and stables, theatres and taverns, everything the people need. Life goes on there day and night, it is never quiet.

"Now look over there to the right. In the middle between the square and the western city gate is Singon Street. That's where we'll be staying."

Barnabas was about to set off down the mountain when Paul stopped him.

"What is that?" he asked, pointing to a large, imposing building that sat on an island in the middle of the river.

"That's the imperial palace," Barnabas replied. "King Herod wanted to model the city on Rome, so he made everything ridiculously big."

It reminded Paul of Herod's palace in Jerusalem and the Antonia Fortress next to the temple. He felt the same distaste for this pompous spectacle as he had for them.

Barnabas was about to set off again when Paul stopped him once more.

"And what is that enormous sculpture?" he asked, pointing to the carving in the rock face high above them.

"That is a statue of Charon the ferryman, who the Greeks say ferries the souls of the dead across the River Styx to the underworld."

"But why is it still standing there now that the souls of the dead are led to heaven by Christ?"

"Because many people still believe in that figure. That is why I have brought you here, so you can explain these things to them."

"Then we shouldn't stand around here chatting all day, let's go."

Paul smiled at Barnabas and started down the mountain at a brisk pace. Barnabas shook his head and followed.

Paul was received warmly by the community and quickly settled into his new life among them. He spent his time telling people about what he had experienced. As their understanding grew, the people began to feel it was important that they call themselves after Christ. And so it was in Antioch that the People of the Way of Jesus first called themselves Christians.

III

The following year, messengers arrived from Jerusalem to tell them about a great crisis in that city. The community in Jerusalem were being persecuted by the Jews who felt threatened by them. Some people had been imprisoned, others had fled, and those who remained behind and had avoided prison were having a hard time finding work. As a result, donations had decreased and poverty was spreading. When they heard this, the community in Antioch raised a large sum of money and sent Paul and Barnabas to Jerusalem to deliver it.

When they reached the city they went to the Essene house on Mount Zion. The people there welcomed them and gratefully accepted the money. But Paul and Barnabas noticed that Mary, the house mother, appeared anxious. Barnabas asked his sister what the matter was and she told them that Peter was in prison and they feared for his life.

That evening Paul and Barnabas, Mary and her son John Mark, and their servant girl Rhoda, as well as a number of the apostles, all gathered in the upper room of the house. It was here that Jesus had celebrated the Last Supper that fateful Passover week all those years ago. It was clear to them that they would not be able to free Peter, and so they did the only thing they could: they prayed to God for help.

Later that night, while they were still gathered in the upper room, they heard someone knocking on the door below. It was after midnight and they looked around at each other anxiously, afraid that soldiers had come to arrest them.

But would soldiers really take the trouble to knock so politely? Wouldn't they just knock the door down and barge in?

Rhoda went downstairs and asked who was there. From the other side of the door a male voice answered. Rhoda was so surprised that she ran back upstairs.

"It's Peter!" she cried. "Peter is at the door!"

"You're hearing things child," said one person.

"Don't talk nonsense," said another.

But then they heard more knocking, louder this time, and they all recognised Peter's voice asking to be let in. Rhoda ran down again and opened the door to him. Peter came upstairs and greeted everyone; he was especially pleased to see Paul and Barnabas. He was given food and something to drink and then he told his story.

"After I was arrested I was placed in a cell between two soldiers, bound to them both by chains. I was fast asleep when a bright light filled the cell and woke me up. I saw an angel of the Lord standing before me. It told me to get up and immediately the chains fell from my wrists. The soldiers either side of me remained sleeping. Then the angel told me to put on my clothes and my sandals and to wrap my cloak around me. I did as I was told and then the angel led me out of the prison. We passed more guards until finally we came to the great iron gate of the prison. I didn't think at that point that any of this was really happening. I thought it was all a dream or some kind of vision and that I was still in the cell, chained between those two soldiers. The iron gate swung open by itself, and we passed through it into the city. We walked to the end of the street and that's where the angel disappeared. I came awake to myself properly in that moment and, realising where I was, I hurried straight here."

Everyone was astonished by Peter's story and grateful for his escape. Amid the celebrations, Peter spoke with Paul. Paul had listened closely to Peter as he told his story, and Paul sensed that in the older man he had found a true friend, someone who understood everything that had happened to him.

Peter left shortly after that to escape the soldiers who would be searching for him in the morning, and a few days later Paul and Barnabas returned to Antioch. Mary's son, John Mark, came with them.

9: Paul's First Great Journey

I

In Antioch it was decided that everything that Paul and Barnabas had told them should be shared with other people in other places, and so the two men agreed to undertake a long journey. Barnabas asked John Mark to join them.

Barnabas wanted to begin in the place of his birth, the island of Cyprus. And so they travelled to Paphos on the southern coast of Cyprus, where they stayed for a long time. They spoke with the governor, Sergius Paulus, about all the new things they had experienced and come to know, and he listened to them eagerly. Paul was impressed by this friendly, hospitable ruler, who very modestly used his own name, Paulus, as a surname. Paul took that as an example and from then on used his new name with more confidence. For he was training himself not to be a powerful person, as King Saul had once been, but merely a servant of the Lord. More and more he felt like a *paul*, a humble one.

In those days, Sergius Paulus had among his officials a nasty, crooked man called Elymas, whose name meant sorcerer. Whenever he had the chance, Elymas whispered in his master's ear that what Paul and Barnabas were telling him was nothing but lies, and when Sergius was not looking he threatened the Christians.

Paul saw through him sooner than kind-hearted Barnabas, and after a few days he confronted Elymas.

"We are speaking honestly about what we know and you are smearing it with lies," Paul said. "You do this because you are a disciple of the devil and an opponent of all that is right. You are deceitful and full of trickery and you work your sorcery in the shadows. Very well. If you love darkness so much you need not be troubled by the light – at least for a while."

Before Paul had finished speaking, Elymas was struck blind. He stumbled around, groping for helpers to take him by the hand. Sergius was astonished by what he had seen and heard and told Paul he wanted to serve his God.

Barnabas was also surprised, for he had never seen Paul do anything like that. From that moment on, Paul became the leader of their group.

II

When eventually they left Cyprus, Paul, Barnabas and John Mark sailed north to the coast of Pamphylia, which was part of the Roman province of Galatia in southern Turkey. The three travellers landed at the mouth of the River Kestros and took a boat upstream to the city of Perga. It took them two days. Boats could not sail beyond that point and they had to continue on foot along a steep path. Towards evening on the first day they came to a flat spot under an overhanging rock. They found some ferns and placed them on the ground, then they lay down to rest. The sound of the rushing waters below and the rustling wind in the trees soon lulled them to sleep.

When Paul and Barnabas woke the next morning, they saw Mark sitting on a rock a little distance away, looking out towards the sea in the distance. He had been quiet for much of the previous day and from time to time he had lagged behind them as they climbed.

"Mark, is everything all right?" Paul asked.

"Yes," Mark replied. "I was just thinking of home. I keep wondering how things are in Jerusalem and how Peter is doing."

"When you have a goal in front of you, you shouldn't keep looking back."

"It's not that, it's this country," Mark said. "It doesn't appeal to me. I can't help feeling that this is not where I should be. Peter once told me about Egypt, and I've been thinking of that place as well. I think you should continue on without me. I want to go back and see Peter. There is a lot I can learn from him. Who knows where he will send me."

Barnabas, kind-hearted as ever, accepted his nephew's decision and embraced him. But Paul couldn't help feeling disappointed and let down by Mark and he gave him a gruff goodbye. The two men would not see each other again for many years.

For two days Paul and Barnabas continued their hike into the mountains. High up, they arrived at the place where the waters of the Kestros rushed out of a cleft between two rocks. For two days the water had come towards them with incredible force. The frothing water had constantly splashed them as it struck rocks and wrapped them in misty veils. In the evening they were often soaking wet, and their ears buzzed with the loud noise. Now, after just a few more steps, the landscape opened out into a wide plain where the river flowed serenely into an immense lake. Around the shores of the lake were towns and villages, and beyond them rose even higher mountains. Paul and Barnabas sat down for a moment to rest, gazing out into all that wide open space.

As they sat there, evening approached. The day became cooler and a soft breeze rippled the surface of the lake. They felt a wonderful calm descend on the whole landscape. It felt good after their strenuous climb.

III

The first major city they came to was called Antioch, the same name as the city they had left in Syria. It was situated in the province of Pisidia and so it was sometimes called Antioch in Pisidia. Just like the other Antioch, it was a busy place. It had many grand buildings, including temples and arches and theatres. It was the home of senators and many other high-ranking Roman officials as well as a large number of soldiers who had fought in old wars.

As soon as Paul and Barnabas arrived, Paul went straight to the Jewish quarter and looked for a weaver's workshop. He asked for work and, as would often happen on later journeys, he received a warm welcome. In this way Paul was able to earn his living in the coming months.

That first Friday evening, Paul went with Barnabas to the synagogue where they told people that they were both rabbis. They were well received and given a place of honour. Guest speakers were something of a rarity, and everyone was looking forward to hearing what they had to say.

The services in the synagogue consisted of three parts. First, a passage was read from the Jewish Scriptures (what Christians would later call the Old Testament), then the rabbi would talk about how different scholars had explained the meaning of that passage. Finally, the rabbi gave his own explanation. The front rows of the synagogue were taken up by devout Jews, but there was space at the back for guests. Anyone was allowed to sit there, including pagans, who wanted to hear what the Jews were saying.

During their time in this other Antioch, Barnabas and Paul were often allowed to speak during the third part of the service.

Barnabas usually spoke first, and everyone liked his honest and friendly demeanour. He said that both the pagans and the Jews were expecting a redeemer, whether they called him Dionysus or the Messiah, and everyone could agree with that. Many of these people had a hard life and were longing for real help and support.

Then came Paul.

Paul began by reminding everyone that people had been expecting the Messiah for a long time, but this time of waiting was now over. The Messiah had already come. He had lived in Israel and had been given the same name as the first leader who had established the Jewish people in the Promised Land. That leader had been called Joshua, which is the same as Jesus. And just as Joshua had led the Jewish people into the Promised Land, so too had this Jesus opened up the way to a new land, a heavenly realm. And although Jesus had died in Jerusalem, the highest

God, his Father, had raised him from the dead. Since then, Jesus lived for all people who were searching for him. When Paul was asked how he knew this, as he frequently was at this point, he told them that the risen Messiah had appeared to him and explained all of this to him.

With each service more and more objections were raised to what Paul was saying, and the leader of the synagogue no longer invited them to come back. But Paul and Barnabas kept coming anyway, for while they met angry opposition from the Jewish people, the pagans who visited the synagogue were eager to hear what they had to say.

The pagans tried to show the Jews how broadly the Jewish Scriptures spoke of the coming of the Messiah, and that this Messiah wanted to be the redeemer of *all* people.

"That includes us," they shouted.

"No, it does not," the Jews shouted back. "The Messiah is coming only for us. *We* are the chosen people!"

The quarrelling became so bad that, following one service, Paul and Barnabas were seized and dragged down into the basement of the synagogue where they were beaten. When it was over they were expelled from the city.

That was the end of their year in Antioch in Pisidia. Despite the abuse they suffered, Paul and Barnabas shook the dust from their feet and continued on their journey. They knew that although they left behind many angry Jews, there were also many who had heard them and sensed they had spoken the truth.

IV

Paul and Barnabas travelled east towards Lystra. After several days they came to a crossroads where they met an old man. His back was bent over as he shuffled towards them, waving.

"Here you are at last. I have been expecting you," the man said.

"You have?" Barnabas asked, surprised.

"Yes. Last night I had a dream in which a man in a white robe appeared to me. He told me to come to this crossroads and wait for two travellers who would be passing this way. He even showed them to me so I would know who to look for. A large, heavy-built man with a lot of hair and an untidy beard–" the old man gestured to Barnabas "–and a small man with hardly any hair and crooked legs." The old man pointed at Paul.

Paul and Barnabas looked at each other. The descriptions were accurate if a little unflattering, but it had been a long and tiring journey for them both.

"And what did the man in your dream tell you to do when you met us?" Paul asked.

"He said I should ask you to come back with me. I live in the city of Iconium, which is that way."

The old man pointed to the road that led away to their left.

"Very well then. Take us there," Paul said.

Paul and Barnabas followed the old man to his house in Iconium. They were each given a separate room. Paul's room had a view of large, distinguished-looking house next door. It was home to a married couple and their fourteen-year-old daughter, Tekla. Tekla's room was on the first floor overlooking the ground floor of the old man's house. Because it was very warm, the windows were always open and she often heard conversation drifting up from the house.

One evening, Tekla was in her room. Her parents thought she was in bed asleep, but she was sitting at her window listening to the discussion coming from the neighbouring house. Tekla had noticed the two guests since their arrival a few days ago and she was especially keen to hear what the lively little man had to say. But her parents told her she was not to go near him or his companion; they were not suitable company. In the end they sent Tekla to her room in the evening to keep her out of harm's way.

Now Tekla could hear the voice of that little man again. She listened closely, fascinated by what he was saying. He seemed to be explaining to his listener how you can become 'completely new' inside. That was an exciting thought and something Tekla wanted to know much more about. Everything in her house was old: the furniture, her parents and their quaint customs, even the people who came to visit. Tekla was young and wanted to stay young. She wanted to know how you could make yourself new again every day.

Tekla decided she would slip out of the house and go to Paul herself.

But her parents had been busy. Not only had they ordered a servant to guard the door, but they had filed a complaint against Paul that had landed him in jail.

Determined to help, Tekla took a golden bracelet and a silver mirror from her cupboard. She opened her bedroom door and was confronted by the servant who blocked her way. He looked at her sternly, for it was his job to protect her. Tekla took the bracelet and showed it to the servant, turning it over so that it flashed and sparkled in the moonlight.

"Trusted servant, if you keep your eyes fixed on this until I am gone, and if you do the same when I return, it will be yours."

The servant took the bracelet and began to study it very closely as Tekla stole down the stairs and out of the house.

When she reached the jail she saw a great big watchman with a big moustache and beard. He also looked at her sternly.

Tekla smiled at him.

"You are an impressive soldier," she said. "But don't take my word for it, why don't you see for yourself."

She took out the silver mirror and handed it to the soldier. In this way the guard was also easily bribed.

Tekla sneaked into the jail where she found Paul in his cell. She sat down at his feet.

"Dear Paul, I have seen from my window how people come to you and have heard what they ask you. I have also heard what you've told them, and it made me think that perhaps you could answer my question. I have only one."

"If I am not mistaken, you are risking a lot for that one question," Paul said. "It must be a very important question."

"It is."

"Then you had better ask it."

"Everything and everyone around me is old," Tekla said. "Not just in years but in the way they think. I don't want to be like that. How does everything in the world become young and new again?"

"It happens through the new human being," Paul replied.

"Who is that? And how do they do that?"

And so Paul told her about the new, spiritual human being that was waiting to be born in everyone.

They talked all night long and Tekla was thrilled to have finally found someone who could answer her question. They were still talking in the morning when Tekla was discovered by her parents who had come looking for her.

"You gave away good gold and silver to talk with a tramp," her father grumbled on the way home.

"Yes," Tekla answered. "But I got much more in return. You can lose gold and silver, but I received something no one can ever take away from me. From now on I remain young!"

V

Paul and Barnabas left Iconium and travelled south-east, eventually arriving in the small town of Lystra. In front of the town gates stood a small temple dedicated to the Greek god Zeus. Next to it stood two old linden trees, their branches woven together.

"Look," said Barnabas. "Isn't that wonderful?"

"What is?" asked Paul.

"Those trees," Barnabas replied. "Do you know the story of when Zeus visited here with his messenger Hermes, and no one wanted to listen to him?"

"It sounds familiar," Paul said. "Remind me again."

"When they came through here disguised as ordinary peasants, everyone turned their back on them, but they were well received by two friendly old people, Philemon and Baucis. They gave them a place to sleep and the next morning fed them breakfast. They also listened to them. Zeus was so grateful for this that he revealed his true identity to them and asked them if they had a wish. The old couple replied that they hoped to always be together, even in death. Zeus then told them to go up the nearby mountain and not look back until they had reached the top. When they arrived there and looked back they saw that the town had been destroyed by a flood, but their cottage had been changed into a temple. When they died, the couple were changed into two linden trees. And there they stand, still together even after all this time."

"So the people here still believe in Zeus and Hermes?" Paul said.

"It would seem so," Barnabas answered. "You can see the temple behind those trees, and the statues of the two gods out front. The large, heavily built figure on the left is Zeus, and the smaller more spritely looking one on the right is Hermes, he is the spokesman."

Paul was not impressed. He made a gruff sound and carried on walking.

The two apostles entered the town and waited by the gates. In those days, in that region, all important meetings took place by the city gates. A crowd soon gathered around them and Paul began to speak. As he was speaking, he noticed a man sitting on the ground with his legs stretched out before him. Paul realised the man's legs were paralysed. He looked into the man's eyes and saw that the man believed he would be healed. Moved by such great faith, Paul called out: "Rise! Stand up on your feet!"

The man stood up. He took a few steps and then, realising he was healed, he began to leap around, crying out with joy. The people looking on were amazed and they started singing and dancing.

Barnabas said to Paul, "Do you hear what they're saying?"

Paul listened.

"The gods have come to us disguised as men," the crowd shouted. "Look, the big one is Zeus himself, and the smaller one, the one with the powerful voice, must be Hermes, the messenger of the gods!"

As if this wasn't enough of a spectacle, the priest from the temple of Zeus outside the town gates now appeared. He pushed through the crowd bringing with him wreaths and a bull to sacrifice to the newly arrived gods.

When Paul saw this, he was horrified.

"What are you doing?" he cried. "We are not gods! We are human like you. It is the God we serve that healed this man. The same God who made heaven and earth and all living things, who causes the rain to fall and your crops to grow, who provides you with food and fills your hearts with joy. This God is a *living* God, not a lifeless statue."

When the crowd heard this they calmed down and gradually drifted away. The priest, disappointed, went back to his temple with his bull.

That same evening some Jews arrived from Iconium. They began to stir the people up against Paul and Barnabas, telling anyone who would listen that the two wonder-workers were frauds. They said that Paul had been put in prison and both men had been driven out of town because of their tricks.

When Paul and Barnabas came to the gates the next morning, they found that the mood had turned against them. They got into a fierce argument and people started throwing stones at them. One stone struck Paul on the head and he fell down. Barnabas went to help him, but he was pushed roughly aside by the crowd. Two men grabbed hold of Paul and, thinking he was dead, they dragged him out through the gates and threw him into the cemetery nearby. Barnabas meanwhile was whisked away by three friends. When the angry mob couldn't find him they scattered and went home.

A small group remained by the gates, however, and whenever someone came and asked for Paul, they replied curtly: "He's lying in the cemetery. We don't want frauds like him hanging around here."

That evening, Barnabas went to the cemetery. He was accompanied by the family he and Paul and been staying with: the grandmother Lois, her daughter Eunice, and Eunice's fifteen-year-old son Timothy. A few other trusted friends were also with them. They found Paul lying motionless on the ground and, at a sign from Barnabas, they gathered round him in a circle and held hands. Together they recited the prayer that Jesus Christ had given the apostles, calling upon God as their father and asking that his will be done on earth as in heaven and that all sins might be forgiven. As they spoke these words they saw Paul begin to stir slowly to life. He got to his feet and went back with them to their house.

One of the friends gave Barnabas a cart and, just before dawn, he placed Paul in it and they quickly left the city.

VI

Barnabas travelled with Paul to the city of Derbe in the extreme south of the province of Galatia. From there it was not much more than a hundred miles to Paul's home in Tarsus. Only the high Taurus Mountains lay between them. After a brief stay in Derbe, they began to retrace the steps of their long journey, visiting the people they had come to know and whom they wanted to see again.

They returned to Lystra where they stayed once more in the home of Lois, Eunice and Timothy. Paul told Timothy about the lives of the kings and prophets of Israel and discovered that the boy already knew a lot about them. He was especially familiar with the stories of the prophet Jeremiah: how he had hidden and guarded the temple treasure, and how he had gone about in the city with a heavy yoke on his neck to show people that they must bear the yoke that was laid upon them – meaning their responsibilities in life – and not shrink from it or run away from it.

Timothy was a good listener and was always asking questions of Paul.

"Do you also have a treasure? Do you also bear such a yoke? Are you a new kind of prophet?"

It was a never-ending stream.

Paul realised that Timothy was one of those rare people who know a great many things in their heart but who try to work them all out in their heads. He never lost patience with the boy and always did his best to explain things clearly. He told Timothy about his encounter with Jesus Christ in the oasis outside Damascus, how he now knew that Christ was a prophet whom death could not touch who had come to help all people.

"Christ is my real treasure," he said. "The treasure in my heart. He is the source of everything I tell people. And the yoke I bear consists of my suffering and the things people do to me, such as the stoning you witnessed the last time I was here. Ten years ago I oversaw the stoning of a holy man, his name was Stephen. Ever since then I have known that that deed would return to me one day. That finally happened here in your city. I did not run from it, instead I let it happen."

"But why?" asked Timothy.

"People who have experienced a great deal of pain in their lives, and who have been able to bear it, in some ways become more human. It smooths their rough edges and blunts their sharp corners. It makes their hearts more tender, and they have a far greater capacity for love and compassion than they did before. Then they begin to be a little like that prophet of mine outside Damascus."

Timothy had more questions, but Paul said that was enough for one day.

"This is my best student," he said to himself. "I wonder how this will turn out."

He thought he knew. Timothy would travel with him on many of his journeys and he would become like a son to him. And that is indeed what happened in subsequent years.

After a few months, Paul and Barnabas returned to Antioch in Syria. The community was overjoyed to see them after almost four years away, and they celebrated their return. Paul and Barnabas talked late into the night, telling them about their journey, the people they had met and the many wonders they had experienced.

10: Everything is Made New

One day, not long after their return, Paul and Barnabas sat down to a communal dinner in the house on Singon Street. One of the dishes was rabbit meat, which both Paul and Barnabas ate, but the Jews did not. According to their laws the rabbit was an unclean animal and a true Jew was not allowed to eat its meat.

"Firstly, you two are not allowed to eat this meat," the Jews said. "And secondly, the pagans who worship Christ must adopt the Jewish laws. Jesus was a Jew, and those who follow him have to live by his laws."

"But everything has changed," Paul said. "Through Christ everything is made new. That is what I've been saying all these years."

This debate had been going on for a long time and it became clear that these differences could not be settled in Antioch. And so Paul and Barnabas travelled to Jerusalem where they had long conversations with Peter, James and John. They told them what they had done and that many pagans and some Jews had accepted everything very well, but some Jews had the opinion that a Christian also had to adopt the Jewish laws.

The apostles discussed the matter for a long time.

James was vocal in agreeing with the Jews.

"Jesus himself was a Jew," he said. "Our people were always expecting him. He is our Messiah, and he died and was resurrected here in Jerusalem. He is completely Jewish. That is why people who follow him must also adopt Judaism. Why should we concern ourselves with those pagans anyway?"

But Paul answered, "Christ came for all of humanity, and in all of humanity the Jews are but a very small people. You can't expect the whole world to adopt Jewish customs. Things have to become much more open. That way many more people will be able to see and understand Christ and be helped by him."

The discussion between James and Paul had gone back and forth for some time. Then Peter spoke up.

"I can see both sides of the argument but let me tell you about something that happened to me a while ago. I was staying with Simon the tanner in Caesarea. One day I was sitting on the flat roof of his house saying my prayers. It was around midday and I was hungry because I had had breakfast early. I looked up and saw something coming towards me from out of the heavens. It looked like a great sheet that was held tight at the corners and in which something was being lowered down to me. When I looked at it I saw all kinds of animals running around, including a rabbit and a pig.

"As I was looking I heard a voice from above say, 'Peter, all these animals you may eat.' But I answered, 'Lord, those animals? I have never yet eaten anything unclean, and all those animals there are unclean by our law.' Then I heard the voice again, saying, 'What God declares to be clean you must not consider unclean.'

"I was thinking about this when someone knocked on

the front door. I went downstairs and found two soldiers who asked me to come and see their officer. As I was hesitating I heard the same voice say, 'Go, for I have sent them to you.' I went with them, and on the way they told me that their officer, Cornelius, was a pious and just man and that he wanted to speak with me. When I came to him, he fell on his knees before me, but I told him, 'I am only a man like you. Get up and tell me why you have sent for me.'

"He told me that in the morning a man in a shining robe had come to him. The man had said that he had to fetch Peter who was staying in the house of the tanner. He would tell him what he should do. Then I understood," said Peter, "that it was Christ himself who had spoken to this man. And also that it was Christ who told me to go and help him. Nothing was said about Jewish laws. That is why I believe that Christ wants to help both Jews and pagans and speaks to both."

This was followed by a long silence.

Then James said, "I think Paul and Barnabas are right. But what about you, John? You have been quiet all this time."

"Yes, everything is becoming different and new," John said. "Jews and pagans must come together in a spirit of equality and help each other."

They all felt that this was true, but they also knew that a great deal would have to change before this could become a reality.

The next day Paul and Barnabas returned to Antioch. The people there were extremely happy with the apostles' decision, and Paul decided to make another trip to discuss it in the communities he had previously visited.

Barnabas was excited upon hearing this news.

"It will be good, the three of us travelling together again," he said.

"Not John Mark," Paul said. "Not after he left us at Perga."

"But I would like to travel with my nephew," Barnabas said.

"Then go with him," Paul replied. "I need a companion I can rely upon, someone who lives up to his word."

Barnabas was hurt by Paul's criticism of his nephew and so the two men parted company. Barnabas and Mark sailed to Cyprus, while Paul chose a young man called Silas to accompany him on his journey through Syria.

11: Paul's Second Great Journey

I

Paul travelled with Silas from Antioch through the villages and cities of Syria to Tarsus, and from there through the surrounding country of Cilicia.

"Now it is time for us to take the trail up into the mountains," Paul said.

The two men set a steady pace as they climbed the forested slopes of the Taurus Mountains. Through the trees they could see the sheer rock face of the mountain towering over them.

"That is the Cilician Gate," Paul said, pointing to a narrow cleft in the rock. "That is where we will cross through to the other side."

After several more hours they reached the pass.

"When Alexander the Great came to Tarsus over three hundred years ago, his army had to go through here. It was a struggle for them and they had to endure a lot of bitter fighting because the soldiers could only pass through in single file. This is an easy place to defend and a costly one to capture. That's why in Tarsus we feel pretty safe from attacks from the west."

Paul and Silas stayed in Derbe for a week before carrying on to Lystra. As they passed through the city gates a man jumped out at them. He shouted for joy when he saw Paul and embraced him. It was the same man Paul had healed when he was last here. He looked strong and healthy. As Paul and Silas walked through the city towards the house of Lois and Eunice, the man walked with them, pointing at Paul and telling everyone they passed that the one who had healed him had returned. Word spread quickly and so it was that Lois and Eunice knew to expect Paul a good few minutes before he arrived with Silas. The two men stayed for a few days and Paul visited many of the people who had heard him speak before.

Eunice's son, Timothy, was now a young man. He had read a great deal from Scripture and knew much of it by heart. Paul was very impressed by him.

"He is more familiar with the Jewish religion than most people," Paul told Lois and Eunice. "And from me he has heard what Christ did. Therefore, I ask you: may I take him with me on my travels? He will learn a lot and later on he will be able to take over my tasks."

Lois and Eunice thought about this during the rest of the time that Paul was in Lystra, and at the end of his stay they agreed to let Timothy go with him. Timothy himself was eager to accompany Paul and Silas.

When they left Lystra, Paul wanted to head west towards Ephesus.

"Ephesus is an important city," he said, "and I'm sure there will be many people there who wish to hear what we have to say."

But the next day Paul said, "I have told you before that I must do what the Holy Spirit tells me to do. This past night the Spirit forbade me to go west, instead it told me to go straight ahead. I don't know why or what will happen when we get there, but the Spirit will guide us; I'm sure of that."

The other men trusted Paul and so they travelled north into Bithynia and Pontus.

But again, after only a few more days, as they drew nearer to the Black Sea, the Holy Spirit spoke to Paul in the middle of the night.

"Now I have been told to go west towards the port city of Troas," Paul told Silas and Timothy the next day. "But let's eat first. We have a long journey ahead of us."

II

The men were tired when they finally arrived in Troas after ten days on foot. They found an inn and had a good night's sleep. At breakfast the next morning Paul was quiet.

"Did the Holy Spirit speak to you again last night?" Timothy asked, wondering if there would be another change to their plans.

"I believe so," Paul replied. "I dreamt I was standing on the shore of the sea and on the other side stood a man. He beckoned to me and said, 'Come to Macedonia, we want to hear what you have to say. We need your help.' It was a dream, but it was also something more than a dream. This is the third time the Spirit has called me on this journey, and so I propose we cut our stay short here and go to Macedonia. Our physician Luke from Antioch is around here somewhere. He is Greek and knows Macedonia and Greece better than we do. Maybe he can come with us. Perhaps someone down at the harbour will know where he is."

They went to the harbour where they finally found Luke in a nearby inn. The Spirit had spoken to Luke too and he had been expecting to meet them there. Luke took them to a ship in the harbour. It was due to leave that morning with a cargo bound for Neapolis, and it still had room for passengers. The four men boarded immediately. As the ship sailed out of the harbour they stood on the stern, looking back towards Troas.

"We are now leaving Asia," Paul said. "Asia Minor is the last part of mighty Asia that stretches far away into the east. Just think: Syria, Persia, India, and China. It is a whole world we are now leaving, and an old world too. Troas knows all about it, for it is the old Troy that Homer speaks of in his *Iliad*. He tells how the Greeks of that time, Agamemnon, Ajax, and Odysseus attacked Troy with their armies and how they could only take it by the ruse of the Trojan Horse, smuggling soldiers into the city inside a great wooden horse. Those Asians were strong, and they still are, but the Greeks were clever, and that made the difference for them."

"Have you ever been to Greece?" Timothy asked.

"No," replied Paul, "but I have learnt a great deal about it. An old school friend of mine in Tarsus is a professor of Greek literature. His name is Kyrill. For three years he taught me about the Greeks. He also taught me to speak the language much better, which will be most helpful to us. No doubt the Greeks will have plenty of questions for us, for they are keen to understand things."

Troas soon disappeared from view and the four companions moved to the bow of the ship. Ahead of them they could see an island.

"That is Samothrace," Paul said. "Do you see those white buildings shining in the sun? Those must be the marble temples Kyrill told me about. Captain, are you going into the harbour there? Can we go ashore?"

"Yes, but not for long, only two hours," the captain replied. "Then I set sail again, with or without you. And if I go without you, it'll be a long swim!"

III

An hour later the ship was moored in Samothrace with its steep bluffs, its waterfalls, and its temples. Paul and his companions went ashore to explore and take in the sights. The two hours passed very quickly as they looked around in astonishment at everything, and they only just made it back to the ship in time. The next port of call was Neapolis where they went ashore, and from there they took another ship to Philippi. Here, the four men disembarked.

It was a Friday, which marked the start of the Jewish Sabbath in the evening. Paul, Silas, Timothy and Luke explored the city and then went down to the River Gangites where they found a group of women who had gathered to sort purple fabrics. One of the women, Lydia, put aside her work to listen to Paul. She became so interested that the conversation lasted until late into the afternoon. She had a lot of questions and struggled at first to understand what Paul was telling her.

"What I am saying cannot be understood by the intellect alone," Paul said. "Above all it must be grasped by the heart. If you would let yourself be baptised, the Lord will open your heart and you will understand me better."

"Baptise me then," Lydia said.

So as the sun began to set, Paul baptised Lydia and the other women in the river, and because they had not yet found a place to sleep, Lydia invited Paul and his companions back to her large house.

The next day Lydia asked, "So is Christ a god or a human being?"

"He is a god who came to earth and became a human being," Luke replied. "He lives as a god in a human body."

"But where is he?"

"He is in every person who is able to listen to him," Silas said.

"And can you hear his answers?" Lydia asked.

Timothy nodded. "Sometimes he answers you in a dream or as you are waking up, or sometimes during the day when you are quiet. You will hear him if you are sincere and really know how to listen."

"And can I also see him?"

"I was allowed to see him, around fifteen years ago, when I was on my way to the city of Damascus," Paul said. "He appeared to me in the oasis outside the city, the most beautiful, most radiant human being I have ever seen. He spoke to me and told me what to do. From that moment on I have been able to ask him anything and I always get an answer. Maybe not right away, sometimes I've had to wait. But an answer has always come. Now that you have been baptised and your heart has been opened, you will be able to hear and understand him as we do, for he speaks the language of our hearts."

IV

In Philippi there was a servant girl who was possessed by a spirit that enabled her to tell people's fortunes. When she was among people she said whatever that spirit inspired her to say. People were willing to pay a lot of money to know something of their future and so she was very valuable to the men who made a living from her.

"But it's nothing more than speaking in tongues," Paul said. "You say all kinds of things that have been suggested to you but which you don't really understand. I could do that too if I wanted to, but I'd rather speak one word from the heart than ten words in tongues. Poor girl! Pretty soon she won't know what she feels and thinks herself. She will be totally possessed by that spirit and just enrich those men who are using her."

The servant girl began to follow Paul and his companions around wherever they went, pointing at them and calling out over and over again:

"These men are servants of the Most High God. They have come to you with a message of salvation."

This went on for days until Paul decided it was time to put an end to it. He turned to the girl and to the spirit that possessed her he said:

"In the name of Jesus Christ I command you to come out of her!"

And in that instant the girl was freed from the spirit that had possessed her.

The girl's owners were furious when they realised they could no longer make money from her. They seized Paul and his companions and marched them to the market-place to face the city's governors.

"These men are causing a commotion in our city," they said. "They are spreading ideas and encouraging customs that we Romans have nothing to do with. It must stop."

The crowd cheered loudly in agreement. The governors commanded the guards to tear off Paul's clothes and those of his companions and beat them. After that the four men were thrown in the darkest cell in the prison. A guard was ordered to put their feet in blocks and watch them closely.

Evening fell, midnight came. The four men sat in their cell, praying and singing hymns of praise to God while the other prisoners listened. The guard fell asleep.

Suddenly the ground shook and a loud rumbling, like thunder, filled the air. The prison doors burst open and the prisoners' restraints came loose. The guard was roughly woken and when he saw the cell doors were open he thought the prisoners had fled. He knew that he would pay for this with his life and drew his sword, intending to kill himself. But before he could go through with it, he heard a voice call out:

"Don't do that! We are all still here."

The guard dropped his sword, astonished. He got a torch and peered into the cell. He counted the prisoners and when he saw they were all there he fell on his knees and asked which god had the power to move the earth that way.

Paul, who had been the one to call out to him, calmed him and put him at his ease. He told the guard that he should trust the god who had made heaven and earth, for that was the god who had moved the earth so that they, his servants, were now free. The guard took them to his house, cared for them and put ointment on their wounds from the beating they had received. Then the guard had himself and his whole family baptised.

The next morning a messenger came to tell Paul and his companions that the city's governors had generously decided to release them and wished them well on their journey. But Paul fixed the messenger with a stern and steady gaze.

"We are Roman citizens. Your governors had us publicly beaten and thrown in prison without a hearing or a trial. All of that is against the law. And now they want to get rid of us without a fuss? I think not. I demand the governors escort us out of the city themselves, otherwise this will not be the last they hear of this outrage."

When he heard this, the messenger turned pale. He hurried back to the governors who hastened to the guard's house. They bowed politely and apologised over and over again as they escorted Paul and his companions to the city gates.

V

From Philippi the four men travelled west on foot to Thessalonica. In the distance they saw hills and mountains. One mountain in particular stood out from the rest. It had a wide base and sides that rose gradually to a broad, flat top. Against the clear sky it looked like a large triangle with its top cut off.

"I believe that is Mount Olympus," Paul said. "If I remember Kyrill's descriptions of it correctly. The Greeks and Macedonians say that is where their gods live – the gods of the upperworld, that is. Zeus reigns there in the clouds and in the lightning and thunder. When the summit is bathed in sunlight – like it is now – they sense the presence of Apollo, and when it shimmers in the moonlight, they feel Artemis is near. Nowhere do the gods live better than there."

"But the people here also believe in a god of the underworld, don't they?" Timothy asked.

"Yes. He is called Hades, after whom the underworld is named. But he is not felt in the airy heights of that mountain. Instead he is experienced in the darkness of the caves of Eleusis outside Athens. In Thessalonica people worship the gods of light, but in Athens they know Hades, and the darkness of the underworld."

Silas, Timothy and Luke thought about this in silence for a while.

"But Christ knows both," Timothy said eventually. "He stood on the mountain in Galilee when God showed his figure of light to the disciples, and he descended into the realm of the dead after his crucifixion. I wonder, did the pagan gods ever come to know Christ?"

"Christ lives in their midst," Paul replied. "He is their leader, for he is the only god who has lived on earth as a human being among other human beings. Christ teaches them how to assist humanity, which is a very necessary thing given that the great tempter is at work among humanity."

"And what does the tempter do?"

"He leads people away from the truth. He is at work even now preparing for a time when he will appear among human beings as Christ did. But whereas Christ wants to lead us towards the light of salvation, the tempter will seek to deceive humanity and lead us deeper into darkness. He will glorify himself above all others, even God. He will perform all manner of false miracles and fake wonders, and in their delusion and out of love for their own wickedness, people will bow down and worship this lawless man."

Timothy became troubled when he heard this, but Paul placed a hand on the young man's shoulder and smiled.

"Do not be alarmed because I have said this. Christ will be there to give humanity strength and encouragement. He will appear to the people of that time, as he appeared to me outside Damascus. Because he knows what it means to be completely human, he will teach us all how to be like him and defend us against the tempter when he appears."

VI

When they arrived in Thessalonica Paul and his companions sought out Jason, a Jewish man of good reputation in the town. They stayed with him and helped him in his weaving shop.

As was his custom when he came to a new place, Paul attended a service at the synagogue. For three successive Sabbaths he spoke to the people there about Jesus Christ, explaining that he was the Messiah and that he had been crucified, died and raised to eternal life for the sake of all people. Paul managed to persuade some of the Jews who were listening and a large number of Greek people there, but many more were angry when they heard what he had to say and kept interrupting him with their objections. They did not want to hear anything new. They were afraid that Paul would cause trouble for them with the Roman officials with all his talk of a ruler far greater than Caesar.

After the service on that third Sabbath, Paul, Silas, Luke and Timothy were seized and dragged before the city governors. This was by now a familiar experience. Jason, their host, was also accused, but he was known to the governors as a good citizen. Jason spoke up and vouched for his guests and their conduct. He took out his purse and placed a generous sum of money on the table before them as bail.

"Take this," he said. "It will pay for any damages my guests may have inadvertently caused by their words. When they are gone I will come by and settle up the rest with you."

That courageous gesture gave the governors confidence, and so they dismissed the crowd.

Because of this hostility, Paul and his companions travelled on to the city of Beroea where they had a better reception. The people there were eager to hear Paul's message and they studied the Scriptures closely to see if what he said was true. But when the people in Thessalonica heard that Paul had started preaching in Beroea, they followed him there to attack him and to stir up the crowd against them.

The Jews in Beroea who believed in Paul took him in secret to the harbour and put him on a ship to Athens. Silas and Timothy remained behind with Luke. They stayed there for a while before returning to Thessalonica, where many people wanted to hear more from them.

Paul later wrote two letters to the Thessalonians, which have been preserved. He wrote that although he had experienced violence there, it had not frightened him. The Lord had told him that in times to come there would be more conflict and persecution, but it was important for the followers of Christ not to be afraid. Instead they must watch carefully what was happening. For especially during difficult times Christ would draw near to them, so near that some would see him, others would be able to hear and understand his words, and still others would be able to help him comfort and assist people who were distressed or ill.

12: The Unknown God

I

Even though he had left Silas, Timothy and Luke behind in Beroea, Paul had a wonderful voyage. He was now on his way to Greece, the place he had learned so much about for so many years. He would hear the language as it was spoken there, the language he spoke in his congregations and used in his letters. It was the language of the great poets Homer, Aeschylus, Sophocles and Euripides, and the great thinkers Socrates, Plato and Aristotle. Athens was also the city of Theseus, the hero who had braved the labyrinth of King Minos of Crete to slay the Minotaur. Paul knew all those stories. But the place that held the greatest appeal to him was Eleusis. He knew there was a temple there dedicated to the old mystery religion, where specially chosen individuals endured all sorts of trials and performed all kinds of rituals in order to enter the realm of the gods. He also knew that the name meant 'the coming one', which he found intriguing. After all, he worked in the service of the Coming One whom he knew to be Christ. Paul wondered what he would find there.

All these things went through Paul's mind on that voyage. For the first time in a long time he was able to think about things, for after many years he was now alone. What would Athens have in store for him? And what did he have to give to those Athenians?

As this last thought rose in Paul's mind the ship drew into Piraeus, the harbour in Athens. Paul looked towards the bustling, sprawling city dominated by its three great hills. The Acropolis was the highest of the hills, with its temples and statues; the Pnyx was where a great deal of business was conducted, and in between these two was the Areopagus, the Hill of Ares, named after the Greek god of war, where the city government met.

When the ship was moored Paul went ashore with the other passengers. The city was about an hour's walk from the harbour, and when he got there Paul let himself be guided by whatever caught his eye. This turned out to be the Acropolis. The marble temples still shone in the sun, but already they were beginning to crumble. Paul could believe that they were once beautiful, but now the marble was dusty and worn by the wind and rain.

"Such faded glories," he muttered.

He noticed two temples that had been built next to each other. In one, Poseidon, god of the sea, was worshipped, and in the other Pallas Athena, the patron goddess of the city. There was also an olive tree growing on the hill. That had to be the tree that Pallas Athena had given to the inhabitants of the city. According to the story, she had created it with a gesture of her hand and it was supposed to be the mother of all the olive trees in the area. It had indeed been a precious gift. What would the people here do without olives?

Paul looked around him at the other two hills and the many houses between them. He asked for the synagogue and was given directions to it. As he walked through the streets Paul read the inscriptions on the various temples and statues he passed. This was a city full of old monuments. Would its inhabitants want to hear something new?

Just as Paul was growing tired of all these grey buildings and statues, he came across a small building with a little courtyard and an open door. He stepped inside. When his eyes had grown accustomed to the gloom he saw an altar in the centre of the room with an inscription to the god who was worshipped there. Paul read it and smiled.

"Now I know what I can give to the Athenians," he said.

He left the small temple and went in search of the synagogue.

II

In the days that followed, Paul visited the various meeting places across the city to speak to the people there. Some didn't know what to make of him and found what he had to say confusing, but there were others who were intrigued by him and so they invited Paul to a meeting of the Areopagus assembly.

"We want to know what this new teaching is that you bring," they said. "It sounds strange to our ears, we want to understand what it means."

Paul followed the crowd to the top of the hill. He stood before them, their eyes fixed keenly on him, and began to speak.

"People of Athens. I know you are very religious," he said. "As I have walked around your city I have seen many shrines and temples and read the many inscriptions dedicated to your gods. I have even come across one small

temple with an altar and an inscription I have not seen before. It reads: To an Unknown God. When I read that, I understood that in your rich city Christ wishes to remain unknown until each person finds their own way to him. For that is Christ's secret: he does not live in temples but in our innermost being. So enter the inner temple of your own heart, and if Christ wants to make himself known to you, you will find him there as I did."

Paul continued speaking, but slowly people began to drift away. Eventually only two were left, a man and a woman. The woman was called Damaris, and the man was known as Dionysius the Areopagite, because he managed all that took place on the Areopagus hill. They each had a question for Paul.

"You were telling us about Persephone, the daughter of Zeus and Demeter," said Damaris. "You said that she had been abducted by Hades and had to stay in the under-world until the true Dionysus came to set her free. But that is just a myth about gods. What does it have to do with us?"

"Persephone is the goddess who bestows joy and beauty and life on human beings," Paul explained. "Without her, life becomes grey and boring."

"But who is the new Dionysus and is he really coming? It seems to me that for a long time everything here has been grey and boring."

"He is the one I told you about this morning. He is both God *and* a man. He descended into the underworld of Hades to shine his light there and to free Persephone."

"Can he make us young again with Persephone?" Damaris asked.

"Spiritually speaking, yes he can do that," Paul replied. "But only if someone wants it. That is Christ's secret: to those who ask he gives them life in abundance."

Now Paul turned to Dionysius, who had been listening quietly to all of this.

"Did you say you had a question too?"

"Yes," Dionysius replied. "I have listened carefully to all you have been saying. You have spoken of humanity and the Holy Trinity of God the Father, God the Son, and God the Holy Spirit, and from the way you spoke I can tell that you are speaking from experience of these things. That gives me confidence. For that reason, I want to ask you why you did not speak about angels? For aren't there many angels and ranks of angelic hierarchies?"

"How many hierarchies do you know?"

"I have heard there are nine." Dionysius answered. "The highest, the Seraphim, are closest to God, while the lowest are the guardian angels of us human beings. I know the names of the other angels, but I can't tell you what they do. A lot was once written in old books, but I would like to know about them myself."

When Paul heard this he understood that Dionysius was a very wise man and he told him all that he knew about the angelic hierarchies. Later, when he was an old man, Dionysius passed on this teaching to his best student who also took the name of Dionysius the Areopagite when his teacher died. In this way the secret teaching concerning the nine angelic hierarchies was passed on from teacher to student, down through the centuries, with each student taking the name of Dionysius the Areopagite.

III

Paul left Athens and travelled to Corinth. Unlike many of the other places he had visited, there was no community of people to see him off, neither was there anyone to accompany him on his journey. He arrived by himself and left by himself. Nevertheless, in the days that followed Paul often thought back fondly to his meeting with Damaris and Dionysius.

In Corinth, Paul met a Jewish tanner called Aquilla, who had moved there recently with his wife, Priscilla, after the Roman emperor had expelled all the Jews from Rome. Paul stayed with them and worked with Aquilla making tents to earn his living. Silas and Timothy came to visit from Macedonia and they spent many long nights telling each other stories of what had happened to them since they had last been together.

Paul also devoted himself to speaking in the synagogue and telling people about Jesus Christ. But the Jews grew angry with him and became abusive. Paul protested, growing angry in turn.

"I have done all I can to bring you the truth, but you refuse to accept it," he said. "Very well then. I have fulfilled my responsibilities to you. From now on I will speak only to the Gentiles."

But that night the Lord appeared to Paul in a dream.

"Take your time here," the Lord said. "Carry on speaking and do not remain silent. There are many people who are searching for me here, and through you they will find me."

Because of this, Paul stayed in Corinth for about two and a half years.

Towards the end of his time there, Paul asked those who had become his friends why they had stood by him despite all the difficulties they had experienced.

"Because of love," they replied.

"But what about your Aphrodite?"

"Aphrodite teaches us about earthly love, but you have taught us so much more. You have shown us the love that

God has for all human beings and how, through Christ, we can learn to love God the same way. That is not an easy love; it makes certain demands. But if you persevere, it is a love that makes you generous and strong. Is that how you see it?"

Paul thought about this for a moment.

"Yes, although for me there is more to it than that," he replied. "Through love I have become completely free, I am able to be truly myself. But through love I am also able to understand others. For instance, if a Jew comes to me I can be as Jewish as they are. If someone comes to me who is afraid, I totally identify with their fear: I feel it as they do, I live it as they do. And if someone is rich and powerful I am not intimidated by them, for I am rich within and strengthened by the Holy Spirit. I am their equal. In the same way I am everyone's equal, and I share in all their joys and fears and sorrows. That is what it means to love each other and have compassion for one another. To ignore your own self for a while and identify completely with others, no matter how different they may appear to you to be. To know others fully even as you are fully known by them. That is why love is the greatest power there is. Greater than hope, greater even than faith."

IV

Paul stayed in Corinth for a while, but eventually he said goodbye to Silas and Timothy and travelled to Ephesus with Aquilla and Priscilla. As usual he spoke in the synagogue. At first only a few people listened to him, but then more and more people came to hear him speak. In the end though, Paul stayed in Ephesus for only three weeks.

"Why such a short time?" people asked him. "You have been to so many places and yet you have spent so little time with us."

Paul explained that he wished to return to Jerusalem to visit the first generation of apostles, those who had known Jesus Christ personally.

"They are getting old, and as long as they are still with us I have to see them and speak with them. But I will make sure that I come back and stay with you for longer."

Paul did not go on foot, as he usually did, but took a ship that brought him straight to Caesarea in Palestine. From there he walked to Jerusalem in three days. When he arrived at the house of the Essenes he found only Mary there. She was beginning to look frail and sat alone in her room.

Paul asked where her brother Barnabas was.

"He is in Cyprus."

"And where is your son, John Mark?"

"He has gone to North Africa. He is an apostle now, like you."

"And Peter?"

"Peter is getting old, just like you and me. The Jews leave him alone these days."

"And what of the other apostles? John, Philip, James, and Matthew?"

"They are around still, either here or in other towns. But come, let me make you something to eat. No doubt you have had a long journey. Stay awhile and rest."

"Thank you, but I will have only a few figs. My sister, Esther, lives here with her son, David. I would like to visit them."

Paul stayed a little while with Mary while he ate the figs she gave him, then he said goodbye.

V

"Saul! Best of all brothers! You're still alive!"

Esther threw her arms around Paul and hugged him tight. As she led him inside her house, a boy of around fifteen clumped down the stairs.

"This is David. The last time you were here he still had to look up at you. Now he is much taller than you." Esther beamed at her brother, overjoyed to see him again. "David, close the front door and lock it. I don't want to see anyone else today."

Esther prepared a meal for them and they sat down and ate. Paul asked her how she and David were doing and how things were in this proud city.

"Are you sure you want to know?" Esther said.

"Yes, of course. Tell me everything."

Esther took a deep breath.

"A lot of people come to our house and tell us about your travels and all the places you have been. They can't stop talking about the many hundreds of miles you have walked all over Asia Minor. They admire you for opening the hearts of so many pagans to Christ, even as far away as Macedonia and Greece. They also tell us that you have helped pagans and Jewish Christians to understand each other better, and I have heard that in Antioch in Syria the Jews who keep the Law of Moses are talking with the Jews who have become Christians. But here in Jerusalem, things have not gone so well."

"What she means is it's an outright war!" David exclaimed. "They can't stand each other."

"I know that you have come for both pagans and Jews,

but please understand, many of the Jews who come here want nothing to do with Christ. After all, he was sentenced and punished by our Supreme Court. For that reason they will fight the Christians. Why else do you think I locked the front door?"

"They are all afraid that the Law of Moses has had its day," David said. "They don't want to accept that people can find a law in their heart that is infinitely more human than what was written down for us twelve hundred years ago."

Paul sighed to hear such news.

"Christ is now worshipped in so many places, and it would be a terrible misfortune if the Jews did not open their hearts to him as well," he said. "I'm sorry to hear there is still much disagreement among the brothers and sisters here. I had hoped to see the apostles during my visit, but I am expected back in Antioch. My dear sister and nephew, it has filled me with such joy to see you again. Thank you for your wonderful hospitality, and I pray to God that it won't be too long before we see each other again."

13: Paul's Third Great Journey

I

The Christians in Antioch were overjoyed when Paul returned.

"Are you going to stay here now?" they asked.

"Yes," he replied, "but only to hear how you have all been doing and to tell you news of my travels. After that I'll be going on another trip."

And so Paul called on the elders in their homes while the younger ones came to see him in the house on Singon Street. He told everyone all that he had done and experienced, and no sooner had he done so than he was on his way again.

Paul set out on foot to Tarsus and from there travelled through Galatia to the western part of Asia Minor. He was reunited with the friends he had made years ago, and he met many more people who wanted to hear him. He travelled from place to place until finally he came once again to Ephesus. When he had last been there he had stayed for just three weeks. This time he would stay for three years. He would live and work there, and Ephesus would be his base for the many other places Paul visited in Asia Minor.

One of the first things the people in Ephesus showed Paul was where the great temple dedicated to the goddess Artemis had stood.

"Here, on the remains of these foundations, the famous temple of our goddess stood. You can still see some of the old walls and columns. The land you see around here was deposited over centuries by the retreating sea. Originally the temple stood much closer to the shore, and the ships that came from the west could see it from afar. It was made from marble and stood out against the dark background of the hills. In the sunlight it appeared radiant.

"Then, one day, a man called Herostratus threw a burning torch into the temple. The fire spread too fast for anyone to put it out and the entire building was destroyed. We still worship Artemis though. The silversmiths and stonemasons make statues of her in their workshops and sell them in the shops in town. They do a good business, too. Everyone likes to have a statue of Artemis, the large ones for the rich and the small ones for the poor. All the pilgrims and traders who come into the harbour with their ships want one too."

"But why do they buy them?" Paul asked.

The local people were astonished when they heard this. Didn't everyone know that Artemis was the great mother of all creatures, and that her forces made the plants and the animals grow?

"That is why sacrifices have to be brought to her so that she will give us a good harvest, plenty of cattle, and our women will bear healthy children. We all want health and prosperity, which is why every Ephesian has such a statuette. We have to keep Artemis on our side. No one wants famine in the land or for their wife to suffer a miscarriage.

The goddess was very angry when her temple burned down, we have to make sure that we don't insult her even more."

Paul heard this story many more times. At first he was reluctant to say anything against the worship of Artemis, but he also knew that the time of Artemis was over and he would not be true to himself and the one who sent him if he didn't mention that. Instead of saying anything bad about Artemis, Paul said that another had come who was far more powerful, and while Artemis may provide human beings with some comfort in this transitory, earthly life, this new god had overcome death and the underworld and had brought eternal life to people.

The Ephesians were highly educated, but even they had never heard anything like this.

"When we die, we cross the great River Styx and enter Hades, the realm of the dead," they said. "No one has ever left that dreadful, gloomy place. Even the singer Orpheus was not able to free his beloved Eurydice from the underworld. Now you are telling us there is someone who is stronger than Orpheus, someone over whom death has no power?"

"Yes," said Paul, "someone who is stronger than death. Like Heracles and Orpheus he descended into the realm of the dead, but once there he let his heavenly light shine into the darkest corners of the underworld. He changed it entirely."

When they heard this, many Ephesians shook their heads and walked away. But as often happened in the places Paul visited, others wanted to know more and in subsequent weeks and months the group around him grew in size. Paul had many conversations with the people in Ephesus, and more and more people developed confidence in what he said. For that reason Paul stayed longer in Ephesus than in any other place.

II

After a few years there were so many people who listened to Paul that the silversmiths and shopkeepers were afraid more people would start believing in Jesus Christ than in Artemis. If that happened then people would stop buying statuettes of the goddess and they would lose their business. One silversmith in particular, called Demetrius, whipped the people up into a frenzy of fear and anger.

"Not only do we risk losing our livelihood," he said, "but if we allow this man to continue leading people astray, then Artemis herself will withdraw her divine majesty from the people of Asia and the rest of the world."

When they heard this, the people poured into the streets chanting: "Great is Artemis of Ephesus! Great is Artemis of Ephesus!" They shouted insults at the Christians, pulling them from their houses and dragging them to the amphitheatre. Paul heard the tumult and wanted to help his people, but his friends held him back.

When the mob had worn out their voices the town clerk came and stood before them. He motioned for silence.

"People of Ephesus. There is no one in the world who doubts that our city has the honour of preserving the image of Artemis, the statue that once fell from heaven to us. Since this cannot be denied, no one needs to get excited. These men and women you have brought here have neither treated the temple with disrespect nor spoken against our goddess. They are not deserving of the rough

117

treatment they have received, and that is not how we do things here anyway. If Demetrius and his fellow craftsmen have a complaint to make, our judges will take care of it. And if there is anything else any of you wish to raise, then you must do so in a legal assembly. Do not commit violence against Paul and his friends, otherwise the city will be accused of rioting."

With these words the town clerk dismissed the crowd.

III

After his stay in Ephesus, Paul visited the communities in Greece. He was eager to see and speak with the people he knew there and to offer encouragement and support. He had been there three months, however, when the Spirit told him that he must go to Jerusalem. Just as he was about to set sail for Syria, Paul learned of a plot against him and instead decided to return through Macedonia. At Philippi, he and his companions sailed to Troas where they met up with other friends who had gone on ahead of them.

That evening they broke bread in the upstairs room of the house in which they were staying, and Paul spoke to them long into the night. Sitting in the open window was a young man called Eutychus. The room was so full that there was nowhere else for him to sit. As Paul spoke, Eutychus grew tired and, overcome by sleep, he fell out of the window. Everyone ran downstairs and out into the street where they found the young man lying utterly still. They were all numb with shock.

Paul was one of the last to come out of the house. He knelt down, stretched himself out over Eutychus and then embraced him.

"Do not grieve," Paul said, to the bystanders who stood around weeping. "There is still life in him."

Eutychus stirred and opened his eyes. He got up, unhurt, and went back inside. Amazed and greatly relieved, the people followed him in. Eutychus was given a seat away from the window and they all listened as Paul carried on speaking into the early morning.

IV

From Troas, Paul continued his journey to Jerusalem. But he was now in such a hurry that he passed by Ephesus and went directly to Miletus. Not wanting to leave without saying a proper farewell, Paul sent messengers to Ephesus to ask the leaders of the community to come to Miletus. Five of them came, and Paul thanked them for making the journey to say goodbye. He asked them how things were in Ephesus and they replied that they still had a question for him.

"What we wish to know is how can we best live peacefully together with our neighbours, our traders, our pilgrims and our governors. As you know, we have many opponents in Ephesus. They revile us because they don't know any better. But how can we protect ourselves and our community against their attacks? You were never afraid. When people attacked you it was as if their words slid right off you, they could never get under your skin."

Paul thought about this for a little while.

"I will write to you about this when I get the chance, for you raise a very important point," Paul said. "For now though, my answer will have to be brief because I have to leave. When someone reviles you and attacks you, most of the time it is because they are afraid. They do not understand you and this make them feel insecure, and when someone feels insecure the tempter seizes his chance. This opponent is not one of flesh and blood, therefore you don't see him, but he slithers into people's hearts when they are afraid and causes them to lose all control. They will throw a torrent of words at you and try to hurt you.

"When that happens you need to protect yourselves. You need a *helmet* to fend off bad thoughts and a *breastplate* to guard against heartlessness. You need a *strong belt* to hold everything together, which means to keep control over yourself. You need *good shoes* on your feet to be ready to go wherever the gospel is needed. When people start shooting insults at you, you need a *shield of faith* to deflect their arrows, and when they challenge you, you need a *sword of the Word* in order to cut through their accusations."

The men looked at each other as they thought about this.

"Please can you say that once more?" they asked.

"Of course. Listen:

> *Make me a helmet around my true thoughts.*
> *Give me a shield against burning projectiles,*
> *With a breastplate that protects my heart*
> *And a belt that keeps me together.*
> *Forge me a sword that knows insight from error*
> *And shoes that lead me onto straight ways.*

"If you say that verse every day, it will make you strong."

Paul looked at his Ephesian friends and saw that they had listened with growing excitement.

"What you have described is armour," one of them said.

"Yes, spiritual armour!" said another.

"Are we allowed to be armoured in this way as Christians?"

"Yes," said Paul. "And we must see that we are. I will write to you more fully about it. Silas or Timothy will bring you the letter."

Paul then took his leave of them.

"I am now going to Jerusalem, but that is not my choice," he said. "I am one bound in the Lord, and I can do no other than the Spirit directs me. I do not know what will happen to me there, all I know is that the Holy Spirit warns me in every city I visit that hardships await me. But I do not let myself be troubled by that. I do not seek comfort. I ask only that I may fulfil the task I have been given, which is to preach the gospel."

The leaders from Ephesus were surprised when they heard him say this, and they said goodbye to Paul afraid that they would never see him again.

14: Paul is Arrested

I

Paul travelled with his companions along the south coast of Asia Minor. They sailed to Tyre where they found a ship that took them to Caesarea.

In the harbour, Paul was approached by the prophet Agabus. He took Paul's belt and bound his own hands and feet with it. Then, in a loud voice, he said:

"Thus says the Holy Spirit: 'The Jews in Jerusalem will bind the man whose belt this is, and they will hand him over to the pagans.'"

Everyone who heard this urged Paul not to go to Jerusalem, but he would not change his mind.

"I have told you, I am one bound in the Lord," he told them. "And in Him I am pleased to be bound. What this prophet has said will happen in Jerusalem at Pentecost. I am not going to avoid it."

II

When Paul came to his brothers and sisters in Jerusalem they were thankful to see him again. The next day he went to see James and the other elders of the church, who by now had grown quite old. He told them everything that he had achieved in Thessalonica, Corinth, Ephesus and elsewhere.

The elders gave thanks to God, but there was one thing that still troubled them. Paul had been seen mixing with pagans in the city, and it was rumoured that in all the places he visited he told Jews to turn away from the Law of Moses. Because of this, a large group of Jews had filed a complaint against him in Jerusalem and were telling everyone that he had betrayed Judaism. At that time, the Way of Jesus was seen by many as still belonging to the Jewish faith. It was an unusual off-shoot, perhaps, with some strange ideas, but it was not a separate religion in itself, not yet.

The elders wondered what Paul could do to prove that he was still consecrated to God.

"What would you like me to do?" Paul asked.

James replied, "There are four men here who must show they are true Nazarenes, followers of the Way of Jesus. They have each agreed to make the offering of three sheep, three baskets of bread, and three jars of wine. Then they must attend temple services for a week. They also need somewhere to live, although at present they have no money. If you make this offering with them and also agree to pay for everything, the Jews will believe you."

Paul had often been treated badly, but usually by his opponents, never by his own brothers. Still, he saw their fear and insecurity, and understood their desire not to stir up trouble with the Jews. Paul bowed his head and agreed. He didn't know how he was going to pay for it all, but he was ready to do as much as he could.

But when Paul appeared in the temple with the other four men, the Jews became angry.

"People of Israel, look here!" they shouted. "This is the man who confuses everyone with his teaching. And now he even brings Greeks into our temple. He is desecrating this holy place!"

They seized Paul and dragged him out of the temple.

Fearing a riot, the Roman commander Lysias marched down with his soldiers from the fortress Antonia. He demanded to know what was going on, but because he could not get a straight answer from the crowd, he ordered for Paul to be arrested and taken back to the fortress.

When they reached the entrance, Paul said to the commander, "May I ask you something?"

"You speak Greek?" the commander said, surprised. "I thought you might be the Egyptian who started a revolt. But what is it you want?"

"I was hoping you might permit me to speak to the people."

The commander agreed. Paul mounted some steps and beckoned to the people to gather around him.

"My dear brothers and sisters, listen to my defence," he said, speaking in Hebrew.

Paul proceeded to tell them his story. How he had studied in Jerusalem at the feet of the great teacher Gamaliel and how he was just as zealous for God as they were. He told them how he had persecuted the People of the Way of Jesus and how, on the road to Damascus, Jesus had appeared to him in a blinding light. He told them how he believed that Jesus Christ was the Messiah that all of Israel had been waiting for, and not just Israel, but the whole world too. And because of this, God had given him the task of sharing the good news with the pagans.

When the people heard these last words they became angry again and started shouting, "Away with him! Away with him!"

Commander Lysias ordered that Paul be taken inside the fortress and beaten and questioned to find out why the crowd was so angry with him.

As they tied him to the post, Paul said to the centurion, "Are you allowed to beat a Roman citizen without a sentence pronounced by a judge?"

Alarmed by this, the centurion fetched Commander Lysias.

"*You* are a Roman citizen?" the commander asked, hardly believing it.

"I am," replied Paul.

"And how did you manage that?"

"I was born one."

"Really? Lucky you. I had to pay a small fortune for my citizenship."

The commander ordered that Paul be untied and taken away, and even though he was still a prisoner, he was to be treated with respect.

III

The next day, Commander Lysias ordered the high priest to call the Supreme Court. He hoped to hear from them what charges they wished to bring against his prisoner.

Paul was brought before the seventy-one men of the Supreme Court. Many years ago, Jesus had stood in the same place; three years later so had Stephen. Both had been sentenced to death. Now they were accusing him.

But Paul did not hesitate to defend himself. When he told them that he followed Jesus Christ they screamed at him.

"Hit him in the mouth!" said the high priest Ananias to a member of the court.

To be slapped in the mouth was a great insult.

"You hypocrite," Paul said. "You act as if you sit in judgment on me, yet you hit me against the Law. God will strike you!"

One of the seventy-one leapt to their feet.

"You insult the high priest," he shouted. "That is forbidden."

"Forgive me, brothers," Paul said, "but how was I supposed to know I was addressing the high priest when he ordered me beaten against the Law?"

Paul's defiance only enraged them further.

Now Paul knew that the members of the Supreme Court often disagreed among themselves. Half of them were Sadducees, who served in the temple, and the other half were Pharisees, who were the scholars of the Law. The Sadducees did not believe in life after death or in spirits and angels, but the Pharisees did. Paul thought he might be able to use this to his advantage and play one side off against the other.

"My brothers, I am myself a Pharisee, a son of a Pharisee. I stand before you on trial today because I know that Jesus was raised from the dead and that he lives."

As soon as Paul said this a great tumult broke out among the members of the court. The Sadducees shouted that Paul was lying, but the Pharisees shouted that it might well be true.

Perhaps a spirit or an angel *had* spoken to him.

The uproar grew more heated and Commander Lysias, fearing for Paul's life, had Paul taken back to the fortress.

That night, the cold, bare confines of Paul's cell was filled with a beautiful light. Lying asleep on a hard, wooden board, Paul slowly opened his eyes. After all the pain and insults and accusations he had endured, this light was a blessing to him. It wrapped him in its warm mantle and eased all his aches and discomforts. Paul realised then that the Lord himself was standing before him.

"Have courage, Paul," the Lord said. "You have spoken well of me. And just as you have spoken of me here in Jerusalem, so you must also speak of me in Rome."

"I will gladly, my Lord," Paul said.

The light faded from the cell and Paul lay back down to sleep. The wooden board beneath him no longer felt hard and uncomfortable, rather it felt like the softest, most luxurious feather bed.

IV

Shortly after this, some forty Jews came together and swore that they would neither eat nor drink until they had disposed of Paul. They went to the chief priests and elders.

"Tell the Supreme Court to ask the commander if Paul can once more appear before them," they said. "He will then be taken out of the fortress through the streets. Let us know when that is to happen. We will then stand ready to fall upon him and kill him."

Paul's nephew, David, heard about the plot and ran to tell his mother. Esther told him to go to the prison to tell Paul. But when David told his uncle about the plot, Paul was not worried. He called to one of the centurions.

"Take my nephew to see Commander Lysias. He has something to tell him."

The centurion took David to see the commander and David told him about the plot. The commander thanked him and ordered two officers to assemble seventy horsemen, two hundred archers and two hundred lancers. They would take Paul to Caesarea that night where he would be handed over to the governor of Palestine, a man called Felix.

The soldiers left the city in the dark of night with Paul and reached the coast twelve hours later. The foot soldiers then returned to Jerusalem while the horsemen took Paul to Caesarea.

The governor met them in person and proudly received them in his palace. He assured them that he had more than enough room for Paul, the seventy horsemen and their horses. He reminded them that he and his court were occupying the palace Herod the Great had built half a century earlier. Indeed, it was a formidable fortress with many buildings and stables. Everyone received their own room.

That evening was quiet and still. The wind died down and the sound of the waves on the beach was a soft murmur. Paul, alone in his room, wondered what would happen next.

15: Paul on Trial

I

Five days later the high priest Ananias and some of the elders travelled to Caesarea with a lawyer to see the governor. They demanded that Paul be handed over to them and they presented their case against him.

"This man is a great trouble-maker and causes unrest among Jews wherever he goes. He even attempted to desecrate the temple, which is why we seized him," they said.

The governor called on Paul to defend himself.

"These men cannot prove their charges against me," Paul said. "When they found me in the temple I had gone there to take part in a ritual of purification in order to demonstrate my devotion to the Law and to the prophets. There was no large crowd with me, nor was I arguing with anyone. The only reason I was brought before the Supreme Court is because I believe in the resurrection of the dead, and of Jesus Christ the Messiah."

Felix adjourned the hearing and sent the high priest and the elders away dissatisfied. He ordered that Paul remain under guard. The governor hoped that Paul might offer him a bribe for his freedom, but such a generous gift did not come. As a result, Paul remained in the fortress for two years.

But his imprisonment this time was not like on previous occasions when he had been locked away in a cold and gloomy cell. Instead Paul was made comfortable. He was given a certain amount of freedom within the fortress and his friends were allowed to visit him regularly to take care of his needs. Among them was Luke, one of Paul's former travel companions. Luke would often turn up with bundles of paper, including two large rolls of parchment.

"What are you writing there?" Paul asked.

"A collection of stories," said Luke. "They're just fragments and notes at the moment, but I'm hoping to join them together to create two much larger stories."

"That sounds interesting. What are they about?"

"The first one will be about the life of Jesus, from his birth to his death and resurrection, most of which you have told me. The other story is about all the things you have done and the places you have visited. It will also include the acts of the other apostles, like Peter, James and John."

"I can understand you writing the second story," Paul said. "You were often a witness to the things I did, and I told you the rest. But why the first book? I've heard that the apostle Matthew and John Mark are planning to write their own versions of Jesus' life. It sounds like you might have a bit of competition there."

Luke laughed. "I don't think any of us sees it like that. It's more like we are trying to make sense of this incredible event and can only do so by looking at it from many different angles. It's a bit like looking at this palace. It's not enough to see it from the front, you have to walk around it and see it from all sides, and then you need to go inside and explore all the many rooms and courtyards.

Only when you've done that can you begin to form a truly accurate picture of it. It's the same with the life of Jesus, only to a far greater degree. It's true that the three of us see eye to eye on many things, but each of us describes the life of Jesus from our own perspective. John is considering writing his own story too. It's the most remarkable story that has ever been told and it needs to be told from at least four different angles."

"And what is unique about your story?" asked Paul.

"Well, for instance, I am the only one who relates how John the Baptist was born. I travelled to the village of Ein Karem, where John's parents lived. I also describe how the shepherds visited Jesus when he was born, and I intend to visit Nazareth where he grew up. There are many more trips I hope to make to see people and places in real life."

"And how do you know what the others are writing?"

"From time to time the four of us get together and exchange stories," Luke replied. "John helps us to understand what we are trying to do. He sees things from our separate perspectives more clearly sometimes than even we can. It really is remarkable. He is always inspiring and encouraging us. He once told us that even if we tried to write down everything Jesus did, there wouldn't be enough room in all the world for all the books that would need to be written."

"That's a good line," Paul said. "You should tell him to include it in his own story."

"I did. From the smile on his face, I think it had already occurred to him."

II

On Luke's next visit, Paul said to him, "You have travelled with me for some fourteen years. You must have a lot of stories to tell about all those people we met and everything we went through with them. I hope you will keep at it for some time to come. But before you start writing again, I want to know one thing. You know just as well as I do that every life has its peaks and valleys, its fast and slow times. How do you see my life in that regard?"

"I have thought long and hard about that," Luke said. "I think that your life is very much like a boat in a strong wind at sea. You know yourself, better than I, that you are often caught in a storm."

"Yes," Paul said, smiling. "But I am always in the middle of it, caught in the trough of some wave, which makes it difficult to see it all clearly, except perhaps for those moments when I reach the crest of the next wave. But they never last long. Can you see what my life looks like from a distance? Does it then look like a ship at sea?"

"Very much so," Luke said. "I see four great waves and four low points in between, as well as a new rising out of the depth to the crest of a fifth wave.

"Your birth took place on the first crest of that great sea of life. It was as if the foam was sparkling in the sun, blowing off a big wave. You were given two very special parents, the great city of Tarsus where you came to earth, and a strong body that could endure much suffering.

"That first wave ran into a valley when, seven years later, you went to school. At first you knew nothing of letters and numbers and all the many laws you Jews have to learn.

But gradually you began to learn until, by your fourteenth year, you had crept out of that vale of incomprehensible things and developed a certain overview. It was even decided then that you might become a rabbi. During that seven-year period you rose to the top of your life's second great wave, and on that crest you saw Jerusalem where the next stage of your development would take place.

"I imagine you had to work very hard to learn the whole history of your people and their laws, and no doubt you felt overwhelmed by everything. That is usually what it takes for a student to begin to grasp what they are learning. It can feel like everything is falling apart and they are failing at every turn, but that is only so they can learn to piece it all back together again. At the end of this seven-year period, in your twenty-first year, you became a leading Pharisee.

"The next high point was a very high one indeed. In your twenty-eighth year, in the oasis outside Damascus, you received your life's greatest task. It worked so powerfully that you immediately wanted to start doing great things. But it didn't work out that way because the ship of your life had to go into the depths again. That was the time when no one wanted to listen to you. You went to Arabia, and when, after that, you still did not succeed in anything you returned to Tarsus and became a student again with your old friend Kyrill.

"Only when you were thirty-five and thought that no one would ever need you, did Barnabas appear and take you to Antioch. There you worked under his guidance for two years, and later he made that first great journey with you. Barnabas helped you to rise up again out of that trough point between two waves, and by the time you were forty-two you had become a leader. You were at the crest of your life's fourth great wave. You knew what you wanted and what you were capable of. You knew that you wanted something different from John Mark and so you chose Silas for your travelling companion. You had also received support in Jerusalem for giving the pagan Christians equality with the Jewish Christians. You even became an apostle, equal with Peter and the others. That was a great step forward. Because of that, Christianity could become a way for all of humanity.

"It's no surprise that after that fourth wave things had to come down again. After your second journey through Asia Minor and Greece you went to Jerusalem for a short time. You were then forty-five years old. You visited your sister and nephew and they told you about the disputes among the apostles and the community there, between those who still kept the Law of Moses and those who wanted nothing to do with it now they believed in Christ. After that you went back to Antioch where you felt more at home, but you didn't stay there long either because you wanted to return to Ephesus. Towards the end of your three years in Ephesus you came down into your fourth low point. The silversmiths made life difficult for you, and so you left for Corinth where you spent the winter. It was there you turned forty-nine. The next year, with the ship of your life all the way down between the waves, you went back to Jerusalem. In that low point occurred everything that has brought you to where you are now.

"That is what I see when I contemplate your life, Paul. What do you make of it?"

"It is quite a picture, Luke, and I thank you for it," said Paul, "I particularly like the imagery of the waves, the crest and the troughs, the high points and the low points every fourteen years. It feels right to me, especially now. For a while I have been hearing a voice telling me that I must go to Rome, and I am going to do everything I can to make that happen. Maybe that rising wave you just mentioned will carry me there, no matter how wild the sea may be."

"No doubt you are curious to know where you will be on your fifty-sixth birthday," said Luke. "Or more likely where you will be on the road, for I have never seen you stay in one place for long. With the exception of the last two years that you have spent in this castle, you were always going somewhere."

III

Felix was eventually replaced as governor of Palestine by Porcius Festus. Not long after he had taken up the position, Festus visited Jerusalem where he was immediately accosted by the high priest and elders. They demanded that Paul be moved to Jerusalem, for they were secretely planning another ambush to kill him.

Festus, however, was a good ruler. He told them that Paul would stay in Caesarea, but that they were welcome to come back with him. He would then investigate the affair in the presence of the prisoner. And so the Jewish leaders accompanied him back to his fortress when he returned a week later.

Festus summoned Paul and asked the Jews what charges they wished to bring against him. When they had finished accusing him, Festus gave Paul the chance to speak.

"Your Honour, no doubt you have noticed that my accusers are unable to provide proof of their allegations. Moreover, I know the Jewish laws as thoroughly as they do and can say with a clear conscience that I have done nothing to break them."

Festus could see that Paul was right, but he also wanted to find favour with the Jews.

"Are you prepared to go to Jerusalem and stand trial before me there?" he said.

"I have not sinned against the Jews," Paul said. "I stand here now before Caesar's court and to Caesar I appeal."

"You have appealed to Caesar and to Caesar you shall go. But first we must hear what the king has to say on this matter."

A few days later, Herod Agrippa II, king of North Palestine, came with his queen, Bernice, to pay their respects to the governor. Festus told him about Paul and all that had been happening.

"I would like to hear from this Paul myself," Agrippa said.

"I will have him brought to you in the morning," Festus replied.

The following morning the great hall of the castle was filled with distinguished guests, their entourages, and castle officials. They were all in formal dress to see the new governor, the king and queen, and this particular prisoner. Festus opened the session by welcoming everyone and explaining the reason for the assembly. He ordered Paul to be brought forward.

"You may plead your case," he said.

Paul stood in the centre of the podium in the middle of the hall.

"Lord King," he said, "I thank you for allowing me to defend myself before you today. Everyone in Jerusalem knows that I am a Pharisee and that I always longed for the Messiah whom God had promised to our people. When I first heard of Jesus of Nazareth, who was executed in Jerusalem twenty-five years ago, I thought he was nothing but a fraud. I persecuted his followers relentlessly. I went from one synagogue to another, seeking them out. Many were thrown in prison and when they were condemned to death I was in favour of it. For that same purpose I was sent to Damascus. But on my way there I was struck by a light brighter than the sun. It radiated all around me and I fell to the ground in fear and awe. Then I heard a voice say to me in Hebrew, 'Saul, Saul, why do you persecute me?' I asked, 'Who are you, Lord?' He answered, "I am Jesus whom you are persecuting." I was then told to go and bear witness to all people of Jesus' resurrection and the new life he had won for us.

"King Agrippa, that is precisely what I have done. I have said nothing more than what was prophesied by the Jewish prophets, namely that the Messiah would suffer and die, and then, as the first to rise from the dead, he would give his light to every human being, Jew and Gentile."

"You have lost your mind," Festus said. "All that learning of yours has driven you mad."

"This is not madness but the plain truth," Paul said. "The king also knows about this, for it did not happen in some far-flung corner of the world, but in his own kingdom. King Agrippa, I'm sure you also believe the prophets?"

"Do you imagine you can make a Christian of me so soon?" the king asked.

"I would pray to God that everyone who has heard me speak might become as I am, except for these chains of course."

The king then took Festus aside to speak to him.

"I see no misdeed in this man that is deserving of either death or imprisonment," King Agrippa said. "He could have gone free had he not appealed to be heard by Caesar."

16: Voyage to Rome

I

One morning, shortly after King Agrippa's visit, Paul was handed over to a captain called Julius who appeared in the prison with some thirty soldiers. He had come to take dozens of prisoners to Rome where they would be used for forced labour. These were men who had been convicted of theft or fraud or murder. Paul was to go with them to face trial before Caesar as he had requested. Luke and Timothy were allowed to go with him to lend him their support. They had seen the fire in Paul's eyes whenever he spoke about Rome and they were eager to go with him. Escorted by Julius and his soldiers, Paul and the other prisoners were marched through the streets down to the harbour where a ship was waiting for them. It was to be a long and difficult journey, beset by bad weather and misfortune.

The ship sailed to Myra in Lycia, on the south coast of Asia Minor, where they found a large ship from Alexandria that was on its way to Italy with passengers and a cargo of grain. The ship set sail with Julius and his prisoners aboard. But the weather, which had not been good so far, became even worse. The wind rose and blew in wild gusts. The crew began to whisper that this could well be the first of the dreaded north-western storms that always made it difficult for ships to sail west at this time of year.

In order to avoid the storm they turned south and sailed along the south coast of the island of Crete. Although they were sheltered from the worst of the storm, they still found difficulty in moving along the coast. Eventually they reached the port of Lasea. It was here that Paul addressed Julius and the captain of the ship. He told them that it would not be wise to sail on in this weather or indeed for the rest of the season. He had grown up in a seaport, he told them, and knew a lot about sailing. But both Julius and the captain thought Lasea was too small a port to overwinter in and wanted to sail for the port of Phoenix further west on the coast of Crete.

When a soft, south wind started to blow, they thought their luck had changed and set sail. But as they rounded Crete the ship was hit by the notorious winter storm. The captain immediately ordered the sails to be shortened so that the wind would not tear them to pieces and for the lifeboat to be hoisted aboard so it would not be lost. The crew even ran ropes under the ship to hold it together. By now, the cloud cover was so thick that it had become quite dark, and with neither sun nor stars to navigate by no one was able to say in which direction they were going. The crew began to fear they might be driven onto the sandbanks along the North-African coast near Syrtis.

On the second day, the crew threw the cargo of grain overboard, and on the third day the ship's tackle and items belonging to the passengers, but that did little to improve the situation. By now the crew were exhausted and there was nothing more they could do except hope and pray.

II

For thirteen says the storm continued to rage and the ship was thrown about on the wind and the waves. During that time, everyone on board fasted and prayed. On the morning of the fourteenth day Paul called to Julius and the captain.

"Last night an angel of the Lord appeared to me and told me that I will soon stand before my judges in Rome. He said, 'The Lord will save you from the disaster and all those who are with you. Only the ship will be lost.' So be brave men and do not give up hope, for I believe this will happen just as the angel said it will."

Julius and the captain were astonished when they heard Paul say this, but so desperate was their situation that they were eager to believe him.

"Nevertheless," said Paul, almost as an afterthought. "I expect we will be stranded on an island somewhere."

That night the crew sensed they were approaching land. Within the shifting shadows of the storm-tossed seas, they thought they saw a darker shadow lying low on the horizon, growing nearer.

They quickly lowered one of the ship's four anchors to slow them down, but the storm was so violent that the rope holding the anchor soon snapped and the anchor sank to the seabed. The captain then ordered another of the ship's anchors to be lowered. Each time the rope snapped another anchor was dropped until all four had been lost beneath the waves.

At the same time, the crew tried secretly to launch the lifeboat in order to escape, but Paul saw them.

"Don't let them go," he said to the soldiers. "We can only be saved together!"

The soldiers cut the ropes that held the lifeboat and it fell into the sea.

Then Paul ordered the ship's remaining store of loaves to be brought up.

"We must eat now," he said. "We have fasted for fourteen days and nights and have grown weak. We must gather our strength for our salvation is coming. No harm will come to any of us."

After he had said this Paul gave thanks to God that they were all still alive and then divided up the loaves.

When dawn came they saw the coastline of an island. They steered the ship towards a small cove where it suddenly ran aground. The waves beat so hard against the ship that it began to break up.

"Whoever can swim, save yourself!" the captain called. "If you can't swim, grab anything that floats. Help each other!"

In this way, passengers, prisoners, crew and soldiers made it ashore.

All two hundred and seventy-six people on board survived the shipwreck, not one was lost. It was just as the angel of the Lord had said to Paul.

III

When the inhabitants of the island saw the ship run aground, they rushed out of their houses and hurried down to the cove. They gathered wood and soon had a big fire going. The travellers, soaking wet and freezing cold, huddled round it to dry out and get warm.

Paul busied himself gathering more wood, but as he threw a bundle of branches onto the fire, a viper leapt out from the middle of them and sunk its fangs into his hand.

The islanders shrank back in fear.

"This man must have committed some crime," they whispered to each other. "He has survived the sea, but justice has finally caught up with him."

Paul shook the snake off and went back to tending the fire. The snake slipped away.

The islanders waited in silence, expecting Paul to collapse at any moment from the poisonous bite. But Paul carried on, unaffected. Upon seeing this, the islanders changed their minds.

"Maybe he is a god," they said to each other.

The governor of Malta at the time was a man called Publius. He came to see the shipwrecked travellers and saw to it that they all had a place to stay and were well taken care of.

Now the governor's father was very sick. When Paul heard this, he went to see him. He placed his hands on the old man, prayed over him and healed him of his illness. News of this soon spread throughout the island and the inhabitants brought their sick and infirm to Paul who healed them all.

During those months, a large vessel from Alexandria was overwintering on a neighbouring island. As the weather improved it made ready to continue its voyage to Italy, and Julius arranged for it take the shipwrecked travellers. When the day arrived for the ship to set sail, the islanders came down to the harbour to say goodbye to Paul and the other passengers. They brought food and extra clothing with them, and when the ship sailed away they stayed by the waterfront for a long time. Paul and the other travellers had been on the island for three months, and they had grown close to their hosts, but it was time for them to be on their way.

For Paul, his trial in Rome beckoned.

17: The Eternal City

I

The ship sailed west and called at the city of Syracuse on Sicily, where it stayed for three days. From there it stopped briefly in Rhegium, a little town on the southernmost tip of Italy, and then continued north along the west coast of Italy. When the volcano Vesuvius came in sight, the ship turned into the Gulf of Naples. It moored on the north side of the Gulf in the harbour of Puteoli.

Paul was still a prisoner, but because of all he had seen, Julius had developed a great respect for him, and allowed Paul to move freely around Puteoli. Paul was able to visit the Christians who lived there and came to know many of them. They were impressed with his courage and confidence in the face of his forthcoming trial, for no one knew what the outcome would be.

After a week's rest, the prisoners set off again. It was one hundred and fifty miles to Rome and they had to travel on foot. It would take them seven days, which meant walking more than twenty miles a day. After two days the country roads changed into a broad road paved with blocks of basalt. This was the famous Appian Way, the long road that stretched from the south of Italy all the way to Rome, the busy, beating heart of the empire.

When they were about forty miles from the city they

were met by a group of people who were wildly waving and calling to them. These were Christians from the community in Rome who had heard Paul was coming and had travelled two days to meet him. They joined Paul and the other prisoners on their march and Paul was able to hear much about their life. After they had gone another seven or eight miles they saw more people waiting and cheering by the roadside, now with flowers and garlands. All of this gave Paul much comfort and courage. He sensed he would need it for whatever awaited him.

Towards the end of the following day, they finally arrived in Rome, also known as the Eternal City.

Paul considered himself to be a well-travelled person. He had seen a lot of the world, including many large cities. After Tarsus and Antioch, the greatest had been Athens and Corinth. But as he entered the city, he realised that none of them compared to Rome. He stared in astonishment at the palatial buildings, the broad streets and the beautiful parks, and he forgot all about the stress and fatigue of his long, long journey.

They were met by a guide who took them directly to the headquarters of the Roman commanders where they were received by the supreme commander Burrus. After the emperor Nero, Burrus was the most powerful man in Rome. He asked about the prisoners and Julius told him what each of them had done so that Burrus could decide their sentence. When he came to speak about Paul, however, Julius did so with such respect that Burrus imposed the lightest possible sentence on him. Paul was still a prisoner, but he was allowed to find a room for himself in Rome. He could come and go freely, although he would always have a guard with him, day and night.

"I suppose it has to be that way," Paul said to himself. "But I didn't expect to have a babysitter now I'm a grown man."

During his captivity in Rome, Paul saw Simon Peter again. It was a joyful reunion. He also saw John Mark, who had remained close to Peter and now lived in the same house with him. He asked Mark what he had done in the years since they had last seen each other. Mark told him about his own travel to North Africa and the many things he had learned from Peter. When Paul heard all of this he forgave Mark for leaving him and Barnabas in the hills above Perga on their first long journey together.

Luke was a constant companion during that time. One day Paul said to him:

"I came to the brothers in Jerusalem from way out in the country, but I was a Jew just as they were. For you it was different. Being a Greek, you came to us Jews like a stranger, but it has nevertheless proved to be a fruitful encounter. Through your writing you have left an incredible legacy for the people who will come after us."

"Meeting you and the other apostles was invigorating," Luke said. "It gave me a new life in so many ways."

"It was invigorating for us too."

Luke gave Paul a funny look, as though he thought the older man was teasing him.

"I mean that," Paul said. "Come over here, let me show you what I mean."

Luke crossed to the window where Paul was standing. It looked out over a small courtyard in the centre of which grew an olive tree. Paul pointed to it.

"Look closely at that tree. Up on the right you can see a branch with slightly different leaves and smaller fruit. That is the branch of a wild olive tree that was grafted onto this tree not so long ago. They did that because the old branch that used to be there was damaged."

"How strange," said Luke. "I always thought it was done the other way around. I thought they grafted the branch of a cultivated tree onto the trunk of a wild one."

"Ah, but you see the olive is such a strong tree that its roots can even cause a wild branch to bear fruit. And the wild branch brings vigorous new life to this cultivated tree, which has grown old. You see, Luke, the Jewish people with their age-old history is just such an olive tree, and we may give thanks to God that a Greek like you came to us. It is good for all of us, for it produces much fruit and ensures life goes on."

II

Paul remained under guard in his own rented house for two years. During that time he spoke to any and all who would listen about the only truly Eternal City there was, not an earthly Rome but a heavenly Jerusalem, the kingdom of God, and he testified to them about Jesus Christ, the Messiah. At the end of that time Paul was declared innocent by the court. Paul jumped up and shook hands with the soldier who had been guarding him.

"I hope I wasn't too difficult," he said.

"Difficult? You were the best prisoner I've ever had to guard. I just hope I get another one like you."

Now that Paul was finally free he picked up his tasks from where he had left off all those years ago, although he had never really stopped. He travelled to Ephesus where he shared more and more of his work with Timothy as he had always imagined he would, and he showed Titus, another of his companions, what needed to be done in Crete. He visited congregations throughout Asia Minor, Macedonia and Greece, reuniting with old friends and making new ones.

Four years later, when Paul was fifty-nine, messengers arrived from Rome with news of a fire in the city. Fourteen of the city's eighteen districts were damaged or destroyed. The emperor Nero, who many suspected had ordered the fire, blamed the Christians and was persecuting them more cruelly than ever before.

Alarmed by this, Paul hurried back to Rome where he found only a shattered fragment of the community there. Many Christians had either fled or been put in prison, and it wasn't long before Paul was also seized and put in prison. Only this time he wasn't allowed to find a comfortable house to live in. Instead he was placed in a damp and chilly cell. As always, Luke was with him, and Timothy was there for part of the time as well. It was to him that Paul addressed his last letter.

Not long after that Paul was condemned to death by the sword.

This came as a terrible blow to his followers, but it was Paul who comforted them. He told them, as he had the elders in Ephesus, that his only desire had been to fulfil the task he had been given, which was to preach the gospel. This he had done. He was satisfied.

As a result of his tireless journeys, he had spread the gospel throughout Asia Minor and into Europe, establishing and nurturing communities in many different lands. Many of them were the same lands his father had shown him in the mountains, when he had told Paul about the

Messiah and compared him to a light that shines in the east and is seen in the west. Paul had carried that light to all those places.

And wherever he went, Paul had seen olive trees growing, their newly grafted branches weighed down with fresh olives.

"I am like an olive tree myself," he used to say to people, "old and gnarled."

He would fix his attentive listeners, especially the children, with a suitably wizened look. Then he would smile and despite his claims to be old, the years would fall away from him. A light would shine in his eyes, and he would seem a young man again.

"But just look at the fruit," he would say. "That's what counts!"

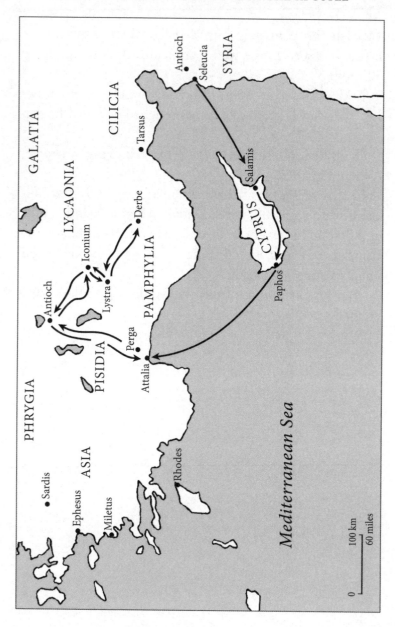

Map 1: Paul's first great journey (AD 46–48).

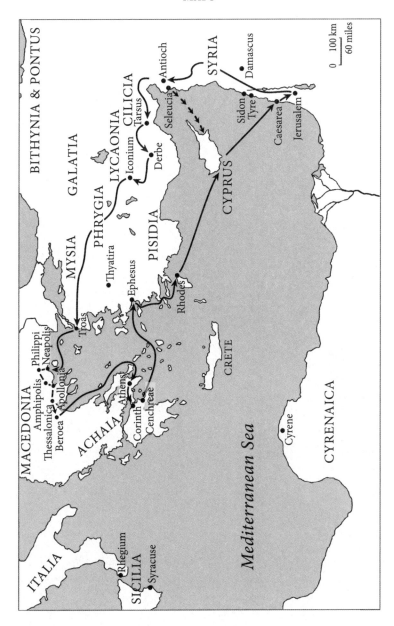

Map 2: Paul's second great journey (AD 49–52).

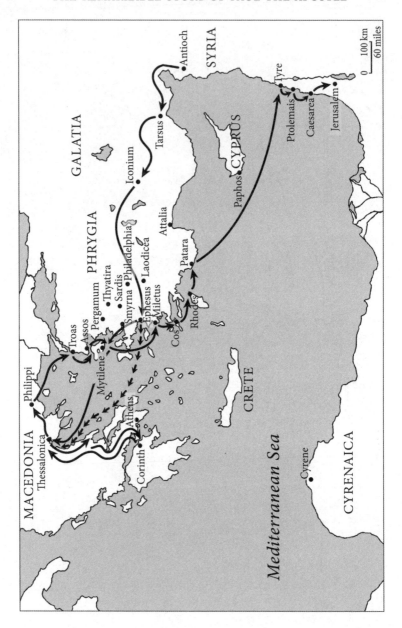

Map 3: Paul's third great journey (AD 53–57).

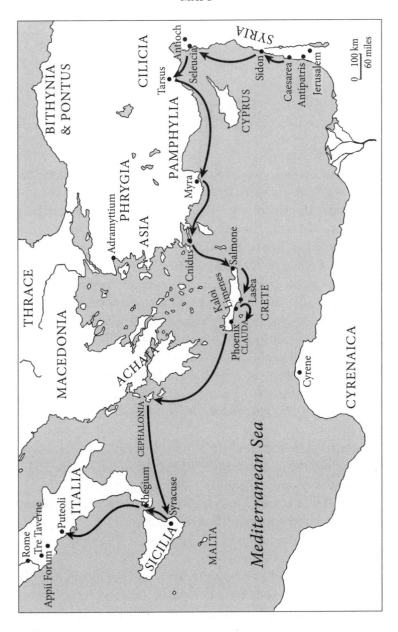

Map 4: Paul's journey to Rome (AD 59–60).

Glossary

Absalom: the third son of King David. He rebelled against his father and was killed by his father's soldiers.

Alexander the Great: the son of King Philip II of Macedonia (356–323 BC). Aristotle was his teacher, and later on he founded an empire that stretched from Greece to India.

Antony: Roman politician and general (83–30 BC). Embarked on a love affair with Queen Cleopatra of Egypt.

Areopagus: the Hill of Ares, named after the Greek god of war. A rocky mound near the Acropolis in Athens, it was a meeting place where matters of politics and justice were decided.

Aristotle: Greek philosopher and naturalist (384–322 BC). Student of Plato and teacher of Alexander the Great.

Artemis: goddess of the hunt and ruler of wild places. The daughter of Zeus and Leto, twin sister of the sun god Apollo.

Charon: in Greek mythology he is the ferryman who carries the souls of the dead across the River Styx to the underworld.

Cleopatra: queen of Egypt (69–30 BC).

David: Israel's second king (c. 1000 BC). According to Biblical tradition he wrote many of the psalms.

Demeter: goddess of grain and agriculture. The sister of Zeus and mother of Persephone.

Dionysus: the god of wine and ecstasy, and the patron deity of tragedies and comedies. The son of Zeus and Persephone.

Eleusis: a coastal town west of Athens. It was the centre of the Eleusinian Mysteries, secret religious rites that worshipped the goddesses Demeter and Persephone.

Essenes: members of a small Jewish sect who lived as ascetics in colonies. One such colony was located near the Dead Sea.

Eurydice: wife of the poet and musician Orpheus. After her death, Orpheus tried in vain to bring her back from the underworld.

Euripides: Greek playwright who wrote tragedies (480–406 BC).

Golgotha: the Place of the Skulls, also known as Calvary. A rocky hill outside Jerusalem where the Romans crucified criminals. Jesus Christ was also crucified there.

Hades: ruler of the underworld, the realm of the dead. It is also the name given to that place.

Hephaestus: Greek god of blacksmiths and metalworkers among others. A son of Zeus.

Herakles: Greek hero and son of Zeus, famed for his many feats of strength. Known as Hercules by the Romans.

Hermes: winged messenger of the gods and son of Zeus. The god of commerce and cunning.

Homer: Greek poet who wrote *The Iliad* and *The Odyssey* (*c.* 750 BC).

Levite: Jewish temple servants, descended from Levi, the son of the patriarch Jacob and Leah.

Messiah: Hebrew for 'anointed one'. Refers to the long-awaited Jewish saviour who will bring peace. Translated in Greek as Christos from which we get Christ.

Minotaur: half-man, half-bull monster of Greek legend imprisoned in a labyrinth in Crete. Killed by the Greek hero Theseus.

Odysseus: the main character in Homer's *The Odyssey*. After the fall of Troy, it took Odysseus ten years to reach his homeland of Ithaka. He had many adventures along the way.

Olympus: the highest mountain in Greece and home to the Greek gods.

Orpheus: a mythical singer who received his lyre from Apollo. Due to the beauty of his music, Orpheus was allowed to rescue his dead wife, Eurydice, from the underworld, but he failed when he looked back at her before she had emerged into the upper world.

Passover: Jewish festival celebrating the deliverance of the Hebrew people from Egypt.

Pharisees: the spiritual leaders of the Jewish people and strict adherents of the Law of Moses.

Plato: Greek philosopher (*c.* 427–347 BC). Aristotle was one of his students.

Poseidon: god of the sea and brother of Zeus. Often depicted with a trident.

Prometheus: Greek god who made human beings from clay and who later stole fire from Zeus to give to humanity. Zeus punished him by chaining him to a rock in the Caucasus Mountains.

Rabbi: religious teacher in Judaism.

Sadducees: Jewish priests and scribes who worked with the Romans in various political, religious and social roles. They were the opponents of the Pharisees and did not believe in angels or in an afterlife.

Sanhedrin: the Jewish Supreme Court. It consisted of the high priest and seventy other members, including chief priests, elders and scribes.

Socrates: Greek philosopher (*c.* 470–399 BC). Considered the founder of the Western philosophical tradition. Best known through the writings of his student Plato.

Sophocles: Greek playwright who wrote tragedies (*c.* 497–405 BC).

Triptolemos: connected with the goddess Demeter at whose behest he taught people how to grow corn.

Zeus: father and king of the gods who rules on Mount Olympus. God of thunder.

Also by Siegwart Knijpenga:

Stories of the Saints
A Collection for Children

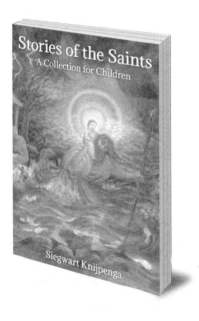

This enjoyable and interesting selection of tales and legends includes over forty saints, ranging from well-known heroes like St Francis and Joan of Arc, to less known but equally intriguing characters from a wide range of periods and places.

In his retellings Siegwart Knijpenga draws on his extensive experience of sharing religious lessons with young people, taking into account what young listeners have enjoyed or responded to, and the questions they've asked. The result is an engaging and exciting collection of stories for children aged between seven and eleven.

florisbooks.co.uk

Floris
Books

For news on all our **latest books**,
and to receive **exclusive discounts**,
join our mailing list at:

florisbooks.co.uk

Plus subscribers get a FREE book
with every online order!

We will never pass your details to anyone else.